T0064438

DEVYANI

DEVYANI

The Vicious Beauty

T.K.B. Sinha

PARTRIDGE

A Penguin Random House Company

To order additional copies of this book, contact
Partridge India
000 800 10062 62
orders.india@partridgepublishing.com

www.partridgepublishing.com/india

Contents

Dedication

To my wife Mrs Kalawati Sinha, who would have been pleased to see this book.

Acknowledgements

I sincerely acknowledge my gratitude to:

(1) Mr. Ram Avtar Gupta, Chairman, Pustak Mahal for motivating me to write about two female characters from the Mahabharata. The first was Draupadi--the Abandoned Queen & the second one is this on Devyani.

(2) My son Priya Ranjan, Director, Ministry of Rural Development, Govt of India and his wife Amrita Sinha, Chief Business Officer, Concept Global Educates Pvt.Ltd. for their unstinted technical and secretarial assistance and

(3) Aseem K. Jha, Under Secretary, Ministry of Finance, Govt of India for constant encouragement.

TKB Sinha,
30 Oct.2015,
New Delhi

Preface

MAHABHARATA—THE GREAT INDIAN EPIC IS peopled with several 'larger-than-life' characters viz. Krishna, Arjuna, Dhritrashtra, Karna, Duryodhana, Kunti, Draupadi, Gandhari etc. Enough has been said about them by various authors. But there are some minor characters who also deserve attention. Devyani, the daughter of Guru Shukracharya is one such character. The episode about her in the epic is not prominent, but the kind of things happening to her needed some 'going into' and exploration. It has a lot of space for psychological analysis and character appreciation.

Evan before undertaking this narrative the very name 'Devyani' sounded fascinating to the author. It suggested a woman of infinite charms, and one who was capable of enticing others by her pleasant manners, intelligence, feminine grace and playfulness. It never suggested anything otherwise that could be termed unpleasant and noxious.

But the Devyani of the epic is different from that of the popular perception. She is so charming, bewitching, inviting and vivacious: yet so ugly, vicious and disgusting.

In her person, at first we find a strong, free-willed girl who would have her wishes fulfilled by her indulgent father at any cost. He revived her first love Kutch to life (killed by the asuras) twice, and then she pressurized him again to marry her to Yayati, a Kshatriya king. She knew it well that a Brahman girl could not marry outside her caste, but her doting father yields to her wantonness every time.

She is so vicious that she compels her own childhood friend Sharmistha to become her slave: although Sharmistha was the daughter of a king, and she herself the daughter of a mere advisor to that king. But she has no moral qualms about that. Nothing pricks her conscience. The only important thing is that she must have her whims fulfilled what ever be the consequences, and whatever others think about them.

Though herself at fault sometimes she cannot forgive anyone for straying away from his/her moral path. When she discovers that her husband Yayati had been having a secret liaison with her maid Sharmistha and had got two kids through her, she flares up and doesn't shirk from getting him punished by her father. It is another matter that the punishment to her own husband (whom the sage instantaneously transforms into a decrepit old man, by the powers of his curse) shatters her own conjugal life. How could she live with a haggard as her husband!! But in a fit of anger, she does it. Anger totally consumes her reasoning.

So this is Devyani—'a fairy princess' transformed into an abominable shrew. The present narrative endeavours to see things in their due perspective.

1

The Rout and After

C LASHES BETWEEN DEVAS AND ASURAS (gods and demons) were nothing new. They had been fighting battles since time immemorial. The only positive thing every time was that devas had always got the upper hand and they carried the palm alone. And it was mostly by virtue of their superior intelligence, their strategy, their belief in their righteousness, and considerable discipline in the rank and file. In addition to this, every god had his own personal attributes to contribute to the event: if the sun god could burn down things with relentless heat, the wind god could blow away things by his sheer force, similarly the rain god could create a havoc making life difficult and impossible: water which is the giver of life was used as a weapon in his hands. These special attribute the asuras did lack. They only believed in their brute force and knew how to use it for getting the better of their adversaries.

As for the strategies and manoeuvrings, it was difficult to say who was the better, but the devas certainly had a clear edge over the asuras. History bears a testimony that in all these battles devas had been victorious. Continuous victories had generated a sense of an awful complacency—a feeling that they were invincible, and that it was useless to strategise their moves in the next battle. Because the result of the same was a foregone conclusion. Complacency breeds inertia and inactivity. It is self-destructive. But this time the story was totally different. While devas were lousy in their move, loose and uncoordinated in their strategy, the asuras were an entirely changed lot. They looked bolder, stronger, better coordinated, better disciplined. They were certainly a different people. "What has caused this transformation?", the devas wondered. It was mystifying.

At the outset the devas fought in their usual fashion with the same time-tested strategy and with reasonable spirits, but they were no match for the asuras this time. Their war cries, their vigorous charge, their style of wielding their arms, and their command and control were looking superior to the devas'. Devas had thought that they would be causing maximum damage to their traditional enemies and would be annihilating them to the last man. And they did it to some extent. But lo! what was happening in the enemy camp!The dead were ferried to the nearby tents, and they were returning there from in flesh and blood, freshly rejuvenated, as fresh as ever!! Every asura decimated, was thus reborn to fight. "My god, what is this!!", the devas wondered. It had made them desperate. Whereas on one hand their own men were being reduced in number, and their strength was gradually dwindling, their enemies' continued to be as numerous and commanding as ever.

It was certainly a losing battle. Death and destruction was broadly written in the wind. Any one could read it. Deva soldiers were continuously looking towards their respective commanders for encouragement and urging them to put up a brave fight, but they were themselves mesmerized by what they were seeing—the dead enemy soldiers being revived, and their own number shrinking fast. The unimaginable was happening.

Never had any deva witnessed such a bizarre sight. It was just unbelievable! Their incredible reverses caused utter disappointment which subsequently drained out their energies. Why fight after all! The enemies were far more superior than imagined. They were just no match for them.

The monstrous war cries of the asuras, their reverberating laughter, their taunts (meant to demean their eternal enemies) further weakened the devas. It was for the first time in the annals of the fights that the devas were so miserably routed. What a shame to the see the asuras chasing the remaining devas, showing clean pairs of heels. Granted that it was cowardly to run away from the battlefield for a soldier, but here all these principles of war were thrown to the winds. And why not? – their own commanders had taken to their heels. After all, life is more worthwhile than those high-sounding principles! When the enemy is so formidable that there is no chance of a win, it is wiser to beat the retreat.

By any account, the outcome of the fight was shameful, sad and unpardonable. Dying in the battle at the hands of the enemy is hundred times preferable to seeking an ignominious survival. The future generations would not forgive their ancestors for such a cowardly act.

The defeat of the devas at the hands of the uncivilized and uncultured asuras had cast a poll of gloom in the land of devas. The air was thick with shame, sadness and sorrow. It had permanently blemished their fair name. They had always returned victorious from the battle field with their heads held high and hundreds of bound as prisoners of war behind them. All that had been negated this time. The dark spots on their fair name could never be erased.

The city of paradise looked deserted, devastated and desolate. It appeared as if an invisible monster had transformed the city into a veritable graveyard: a graveyard—sans activity, signs of life, mirth and happiness.

Where had all the people disappeared after all? Hiding in their digs?

2

A Kingdom without King

L IKE TIME, LIFE TOO GOES on: it cannot stay still as
stillness is but death.. So was the everyday life in the
kingdom of gods—slowly but surely returning to normal.
The thoroughfares and the streets which had presented
a deserted look all these weeks, were now experiencing
footfalls. Business in the marketplace was limping to its usual
pace. People were meeting their friends and acquaintances
after a long gap. They were sporting their usual smiles
across their face while greeting each other. But despite
all this apparent bonhomie, there was an undercurrent of
melancholic reservation, a sort of unknown fear and anxiety
in their eyes. What was it that each one was trying to hide
from the other? Every one felt it, but would not voice.

"How are you, Shriman?"

"Fine", the first one replied. "Times seem to have
changed, Shriman."

"How's that? I don't see any change!"

"No dear, your eyes seem to be saying something different.."

"Of course not, dear. The feeling is related to the state of our mind. The days are the same; no difference at all."

"All right sir. There's a rumour in some quarters of our land that our king, Lord Indra has left the kingdom for an unknown place. And there's none to rule over the kingdom."

The second soul looked agreeable. "Yes, I too have heard something like that. But no one is sure of it."

"Shriman, the ways of the kings are different from ours. They are at a liberty to do things as they like. They may go out for hunting, meeting the neighbourhood princes or just to a pleasanter station to beat their monotony. It may be something like this."

"No dear. If he goes out on any such visits or expeditions, he always carries a faithful band of followers and attendants with him. And such trips are known to the palace people and the officials."

"Yes, that's correct. But what's is the reason of your anxiety? And how come, you think so?"

"One of my acquaintances who happens to be a high dignitary in the administration, told me that the king had left the palace without letting anyone know where he was going, how long he would be away and why was he doing so."

"May be that what you have heard is true. But don't you think that it is bizarre of a king to have left his country to its own fate and go away to an undisclosed destination without telling anyone?"

"Of course it is. A king is after all the protector of his subjects, their provider, their defender and a father-figure. How can he be so indifferent and irresponsible!"

"What is worrisome is that no one knows who will replace him, look after his people in his absence, and for how long. What will happen if an emergency befalls and his protection is sought? And who knows when an emergency may befall."

"Yes such a thing as this is disastrous and unheard of yet. But everyone feels that our lord couldn't be so irresponsible and indifferent to the people's welfare. A king after all is acutely aware of his duties and responsibilities towards the state. He should not be so irresponsible and reckless."

The duo, engrossed in the talk, didn't notice when another soul had joined them. Actually while passing by the spot, he had smelt what their discussion was going about. In these two, he had found kindred souls and wished to share his own views. The first two eyed him suspiciously but soon realized that whatever they were talking was not limited only to them. It was a general feeling. How could people come to know others' feelings and sentiments unless they opened themselves to others? Talking to others generates confidence and fellow-feeling. It also enriches the listeners.

The third said, "You all may be wondering what compelled the king to take such a bizarre step. But I know for sure why he did so."

Both the listeners looked curiously in his face. How come that he was sure of what he knew. They voiced their curiosity.

"One of my cousins works in the king's apartments. He has an access even to the inner apartments of the king."

The two looked flabbergasted. This person must be knowing the truth.

"My cousin told me that the king was vastly devastated by his defeat in the battle with the asuras. He felt deeply ashamed and humiliated because in none of the battles in the past, the devas had been defeated. They always had an upper hand: victory had become a matter of habit.

"The king would often be seen shrunken within himself, brooding in a secluded corner. It was the rudest blow in his life. It was something he could not cope with and digest.

"On several occasions I noticed his loving queen Sachi, reasoning with him and trying to soothe him. In a battle, some one had to lose and some one had to win. Hadn't he won all the battles in the past? Hadn't asuras lost all the previous battles? Why then should one defeat be allowed to negate the earlier victories? It was just not desirable. He should take the loss sportingly, analyse the shortfalls, the deficiencies and also critically view the factors which helped his enemies win.

"But the king wouldn't be soothed. He had taken the reverses as rather too personal. He said that he desired to move away from the hurly burly of the palace life to a far away place, where none could find him. He wanted to meditate, practise penance and please the superior gods for their guidance and direction. He wanted to regain the original strength which the defeat had totally sapped."

The third speaker sounded so convincing and genuine. May be he had the real information. They all dispersed from there satisfied. But the question remained, where had the king gone after all? And for how long? The information about the time of his return was extremely vital. Only this could restore the people's faith in the administration.

3

Wanted—a king

MONTHS OF ENQUIRIES ABOUT LORD Indra's whereabouts had yielded nothing. All sorts of rumors were afloat in the air: but none could vouch for any. How could one? Some one said that he had gone to the 'patal lok'(the nether world) and was wandering there incognito. Some one opined that he had gone to an 'adrishya lok'(an unknown world) and there he was meditating and offering penance, some one said that he was in the 'rishi lok' (the world of the sages) for their blessings and wise guidance. Only those elevated souls could grant real peace to his troubled soul.

But all these were wild guesses. A guess is made in the absence of concrete facts. It is a mere figment of imagination. Only the queen knew where he was and how long would he be away. He had actually gone to 'Prithvi lok' (the earth) and was staying in a 'kamal van'(the lotus forest). It was the most appropriate place for his wounded soul. There were lakes, flowers, fruit trees, birds, beasts and some ashramites (dwellers of an Ashram) there. None knew who he was, and why and from where he had come. In the world, people are free to go anywhere in search of the Supreme Being and for 'tapasya'. For other souls there, our Lord was just another seeker. He was welcome to them, and quite often they would meet and share their experiences and thoughts related to their progress on the path of spirituality.

The king found this corner of Prithvilok to be real heaven. Who would not like to stay here till eternity? The peace of mind and happiness one got here, could not be bartered with anything in the universe. The king had lost the count of time since he had been here, and also he had no desire to repair to his original world. That world was full of responsibilities, duties, anxieties, rewards and punishments. They rob the life of its heavenly bliss. Who was so vile as to spar 'amrit' with 'vish' (exchange the divine nectar with poison)?

⎯⎯⎯⎯⎯◈◈◈⎯⎯⎯⎯⎯

The long absence of the king from the kingdom was making the people restive. It was further aggravated by the fact that no one knew, where he had gone and when would he be back. The king's throne can't remain vacant indefinitely. Some one had to be there to rule over the subjects. A king was not only the head of the state, he was also the guardian of the people, the protector of the land and provider to his subjects. As a father he had also to discipline his rowdy subjects and punish them according to their faults. The virtuous looked to him for affection and encouragement.

The thought of the power vacuum at the centre was causing severe anxiety to the grey heads of the land. This also included the officers in the administration.

"What should we do, Sir?" enquired a group of the king's well- wishers of the wisest soul. But the poor guy was himself as much ignorant as they were. What could he say? Something can be said with certainty and authority, if the factors involved are visible and concrete.

Sensing his inability to utter anything, they said, "Honourable sir, now that we are unable to find an answer to our anxious query from you (it's none of your fault though), we ought to seek the advice from some one superior to us."

"Yes, yes, that's a good idea." The wisest then felt lighter at the suggestion. It would be relieving him of the problem too." But who do you all wish to speak to?"

"We must seek the guidance from Lord Brahma, the creator of the universe. He must be posted with our problem."

"Dear friends, well thought! Being a father-figure himself, he will certainly take us out of the woods. If you deem it fit, I too would like to go with you."

"Venerable sir, we were just thinking of placing this proposal before you. It's great that you've offered yourself on your own. Being the senior most amongst us, you are the fittest to lead the delegation. Even otherwise, going without you to meet the Lord was unbecoming."

"All right, dears. We shall proceed quite early tomorrow."

<hr>

Lord Brahma was well aware of the goings-on in the devas' kingdom. He was himself concerned about its administration, peace and tranquility, law and order. Graciously he granted them a sympathetic audience. The visitors' anxieties were not extraordinary, but commonplace.

"Dear devas, I am aware of your anxieties. They are genuine. An alternative has to be found out. If there is a vacuum at the centre, things will soon disintegrate. There must be a force to tug and tie the diverse elements in nature.

"Find out a ruler from amongst yourselves. And if that be not practicable, seek someone from another 'lok' (world) who can fill up the gap. But be sure to judge his credentials and abilities.", uttered the Supreme Lord with a gentle smile.

"Venerable Lord, we are all beholden to you for hearing us and providing solace with guidance. Your advice will be followed to the letter", saying so the delegation came back to the kingdom.

A frantic search for a suitable replacement of Indra began soon. A council of the grey heads and the respectables in the kingdom, was meeting to discuss the problem on hand. They considered the sun god 'Surya', the wind god 'Vayu', the fire god 'Agni', the divine builder 'Vishwakarma', the lord of Dharma- Dharmaraj but opinions varied on every name. Majority of the learned and experienced opined that each of these persons had already got their duties assigned to them, which were vital for the creatures of the universe. Their hands were already full. Adding the administration of the vast kingdom would dilute their efforts and would do good to none. A king's job is more diverse and time-consuming in nature. It could not be made a part-time engagement.

Finding no suitable personage in 'devlok', the assembly considered names from other 'lokas.'(worlds). The only one which seemed to qualify— was that of King Nahush of Prithvilok. He satisfied the members on all counts. But how could a man from Prithvilok, an inferior world, and a world of mortals be the king of 'devlok'? How could a mere mortal rule over devas—the divine creatures? The thought was not only bizarre and disgusting but sounded sacrilegious.

"Such a thing had never been heard," some one muttered.

"Yes, but such an occasion too had never occurred before. Can you cite an instance when the ruler slinks out of the capital without any intimation, even to his own guards and close officials?"

"No sir, never."

"Remember dears. An extraordinary situation warrants an extraordinary solution. And in the present circumstances, we must not be guided by the meaningless principles and customs which hold no weight. We have to get our ruler, whosoever he may be, and from wherever he may be. One's caste, creed and social status must not be a hindrance to a sacred cause.

"If we haven't been able to find out a suitable person from our own stock, does it follow that we would have none? Let our reasons be not coloured by our prejudices. Gold is gold wherever it is. It must be picked up and accorded its due recognition. That's all.."

"The royal priest's words were well articulated and went down well with the listeners. No one had anything otherwise to say. Actually they had hit a blind wall beyond which there was no movement. It was therefore, decided that king Nahush would be made their king for the time being. It was also decided to invite him to come to Devlok for coronation. And for that a delegation of wise persons would visit Prithvilok and ceremoniously escort him here."

4

The Ascension

WHO HAD EVER HEARD OF a mortal invited by gods themselves to rule over them in heaven? It was beyond the wildest imagination. But it is said that sometimes by quirk of fate, even impossible things become commonplace.

King Nahush couldn't believe his ears when the delegation from heaven conveyed to him their decision. And so were wonder-struck the courtiers in his assembly. What's this my God!! Gods coming to the earth to invite their king to go to 'Swarg' to rule there? Has a mortal ever ruled in heaven? A god's coming to the earth to rule over the mortals was believable and conceivable, but not the otherwise. If this impossible had become possible, then anything was possible in the universe. Strange are the ways of the Creator!

The invitation to the king to ascend to 'Swarg' was not an ordinary event. It suggested many things—either Lord Indra had abdicated the throne on his own or he had been dislodged: either he had been severely incapacitated or he had left the palace for an unknown place. But all these possibilities gave rise to other questions. Why after all, any of these could happen? It had left the people to wild guesses. Whatever had happened or was happening was simply mind-boggling.................

But how long would king Nahush officiate there? The answer was not clear: may be a week, a few months or even a few years. It all depended on how the situation developed. Then what would happen here in his absence? The visitors made it clear that the king was at liberty to visit his own kingdom on Prithvi as and when he wished. After all his own people, his own country were his top most priority.

The Prithvi-dwellers were proud of their kin's selection for the heaven's assignment. He was indisputably the most competent person in the whole of the universe. Decision to invite someone from the mortal world to rule over devas— the immortal, was without any example. For the people their king was wise and just who ruled sensibly, but they had never thought that he was so able, so competent and so famous.

5

Fall from the Meteoric Heights

I F ONE COULD CITE THE case of a real 'wind fall', it was in the meteoric rise of the king Nahush. Who would ever imagine of a mortal from the earth to be unanimously selected by the devas of 'swarg' (heaven) themselves to select him as their ruler? It was beyond even the wildest imagination. Such a stroke of good luck was like the proverbial 'cloud burst'. And it was reason enough to make even the sanest person swollen-headed. And Nahush was only a simple mortal, not a sage, who treats both pleasures and pain with equanimity.

When the grey heads from the heaven approached him with their proposal, he was initially dumb-struck, and so were those present in the royal court. It took them some time to sink in. But the king steadied himself and prepared for the journey to 'Swarg'. After passing on the necessary administrative instructions to his officials, he took leave of all including the queen and his family members. The only saving grace was that he was not leaving them for good, but would be visiting his people and his family off and on.

The gate of the heaven presented a unique spectacle. A large number of people, consisting of women and children had lined up the highway, leading from the gate to the Capital. Every one was curious to see what sort of person their guest king was, what he looked like and whether he would be able to deliver the goods. From a distance they could see king Nahush, escorted by the delegates proceeding towards the gate, entering it and then passing through it. They enthusiastically welcomed their new king and showered flower petals along the path. He appeared to be satisfying their enquiries and expectations.

For Nahush, the things here too were similar. The system of administration follows almost the same track everywhere, because the problems facing it are universal. After his formal coronation, he adorned the royal chair and was briefed about the state of affairs by different officials. His grasp of the situation impressed one and all.

Although Nahush appeared outwardly to be unaffected by his meteoric rise i.e., from the earth to heaven, in the hearts of his heart, he had a feeling of tremendous superiority, which later on was reflected in his arrogance. He had started treating his officials including even the grey-headed advisors with an apparent disdain.

While the daily hours of his business both in the court as well as in the royal apartments occupied his time, he sometimes missed his queen and his family members. He must have some one as consort to share his intimate moments. But his wishes were impracticable.

At the conclusion of his introduction to the officers and courtiers, he was ceremoniously introduced to the members of the 'run-away' Indra's family and attendants. He could not forget his meeting with queen Sachi. She was so inviting and voluptuous. He fervently wished his own spouse had been like her. Ironically, long separation from Indra had not wilted her. It had rather added to her charms. She was just bewitching! He could notice a typical wistfulness in her eyes…………..

It is difficult to deal with loneliness. After the day's work is done and one retires to the bed at night, he is subjected to various pleasant and unpleasant thoughts and also given to fantasies. Unknown cravings torment him. That's the time he seeks some one to share his innermost thoughts. He was surprised to find that the queen of the previous incumbent had started dominating his nocturnal fantasies. He shrugged such thoughts initially, but in course of time they got better of him. The desire to have her with him strengthened with every passing day. But wasn't it unethical and immoral? Of course, it was, but sometimes indecent wishes overwhelm a person and propel him to realize them.

The king let himself be moved in this regard and found himself giving in. As a ruler, he thought it was his duty to also meet the deserted royal family from time to time, and enquire about their well being. But in course of time, he found himself getting increasingly intimate with the queen. It gave him an indescribable pleasure. At times he made oblique references to a separate meeting with her, which were later followed by subtle overtures. Out of decency, the queen responded dispassionately, although she detested them inwardly. Even from a strategic viewpoint, she could not be rough with him. Her apparent sympathetic responses, emboldened him. To him the lady appeared to be a willing partner in the adventures. But a lady cannot be so indiscreet as to voice her innermost desires. She would do it only by signals.

Persistent pestering by the king was fast becoming annoying and intolerable. And now a days it was bordering on some sort of aggression. Sachi always wished Indra had been here and provided protection against the pestering lecher. Her mild refusals and protests had further emboldened him. Finding the situation uncontrollable, the helpless lady ultimately decided to do what Indra had advised her never to do, that is, to seek him in the undisclosed part of the world, as he did not want to be disturbed in his search for himself. But now that everything was at stake, she had no option but to violate the sacred covenant and approach him for succor. She therefore, left the palace secretly on a moonless night along with her reliable maid and reached the place sooner than expected.

Indra was astonished at the unexpected arrival of Sachi. But his experienced eyes could easily make out that things were not well there, and she had been compelled by the circumstances to take this step. Had things been normal, she won't have disturbed him, as she was well aware of the purpose of her husband. It was vital for him to realize himself and seek Lord Brahma's blessings.

Sachi's eyes told of her sufferings, her anxieties and the state of her disturbed soul. It was a matter of real concern. But what could ail a queen? What had compelled her to undertake this forbidden journey? Surely it was something extraordinary. In course of talk with her, he could learn what all was happening in heaven, how the king whom the sages had selected for ruling over them had turned into a man-eater only after a few months. To Indra, a mortal from the earth had vitiated the purity of heaven's environment. And the longer he stayed there, the more irretrievable damage would be done to the society there. But corrective measures needed time and patience. It could not be done instantaneously. But there was a rub: the measures taken by him from here would leak out his whereabouts, and he won't be able to achieve what he had come for. If the protection of the refined culture of the heaven was the crying need of the hour, so was his meditation and penance. He had only a few days left for realizing his dream. Till then temporary measures could be taken to arrest the deterioration.

His first task was to assuage the hurt of his royal spouse. She had been severely shaken and hurt. In her own way she had felt that she could not handle the situation herself. It was impossible to survive in the terror-ridden environment. There could be an onslaught on her any moment.

<hr>

It was a balancing act for her husband: on one hand he had to instill into her a sense of total security amidst her perceived threats, and on the other he had to refurbish himself to enable him to rule over his kingdom. In the present circumstances the best course was to keep the things on hold, as by that time he would be reaching there himself. And then there would be nothing like this. Therefore, he decided to soothe his anxiety-ridden spouse. Taking her in a warm embrace he said, "My love, I am utterly grieved to learn of your suffering and the emotional turmoils you have been subjected to. But remember, you are no ordinary person. You are the queen, the royal consort of Indra, the king of devas. Why should you lose your heart so soon and feel helpless like an ordinary human?

Looking lovingly into his affectionate eyes, she said, "My lord, only the abundance of your love has given me the necessary strength to sustain myself, otherwise I would have broken down." She felt her man patting her back with affectionate and loving hands. It felt so reassuring. She wished he had held her a little longer, but how long would be long enough!!

"My love, you don't have to worry for long. I shall be there at the earliest. Your restlessness disturbs me. I am going to hasten the fulfillment of my mission."

By this time both were sitting face to face. Holding her wilted visage in his hands, Indra looked into her eyes and said, "I repeat, the days of your sufferings and grief are counted few. They will end very soon, rather sooner than expected."

"How is that, my lord?" She could notice a sudden flash in his eyes. Did he have the rush of a plan?

"My dear, listen carefully to what I am going to say. But for implementing the plan you have to act. You have to be a different person for the time being. If that be done, that lecher would crash to earth with a loud bang, on his own."

Sachi looked bewildered. What was he saying? It sounded mystifying and puzzling. She looked curiously towards him for his reply.

"My love, I know, you are foxed and wondering what am I up to. But be rest assured that my plan, executed through you, will put a final curtain on your hardships and his devilish rule."

"What's it, my lord? Please don't tax my muddled brain any more. Be specific. How could my steps liberate me for ever?"

"My love, I am coming to it. You say that the lecher is after you and is dying to get you into his arms. Isn't it? That's fine. That ensures his undoing?"

She looked as much bewildered and wide-eyed as ever. Her husband's secret plan had intrigued her. But what was it?

Indra continued, "After your return from here, act as a totally different person. Don't reject his amorous overtures and advances. Contrary to it, by sending occasional furtive glances matched with your body language, give him an impression that now you cherish to be his partner. Pleased beyond imagination by your supposed consent, he would like to know when and where could the meeting take place."

The queen grew impatient at this. How could all this be faked? She felt herself incapable of playing a double game. Acting was not her cup of tea.

"Don't worry dear. All this will be done without causing any harm to your person in any way. Up till now he hasn't even touched you, so why panic?"

Sachi looked slightly detensed. Her frayed nerves were getting soothed. She looked at him for his further words.

"Once he has been trapped by your bewitching charms and thinks that you have consented to have good times with him, he would lap up every nonsense you care to utter. Then tell him that on the coming moonless night you would be waiting for him at the Royal resort at the foot of the hill. He must make it a point to reach there by sun down, as the resort gate closes at the sunset. But he must come there not by the royal chariot but by a palanquin, borne by the 'Saptarshis' (the venerable seven sages) on their shoulders."

"Then what, my lord? Supposing he succeeds in doing what I demand?"

"Worry not, dear. This will never happen. He will never reach the appointed resort. And because he will never be able to make it, there is no need for you to go there. Actually all this while you will continue sitting in the warmth of your chamber while he travels in the palanquin."

Sachi was not convinced of the success of the plan. But her husband sounded so sure, as if he were seeing the things happening before his own eyes.

"So my dear, there's no reason to worry on this count. His days are numbered, but that depends on how fast you act and manage. As for my side, the plan is foolproof and there is no reason to doubt. It will go the way, I anticipate. It will never misfire, I tell you."

Indra's words seemed to have mesmerized her. She had started feeling some difference in her mental make up. She was convinced, assured and hope-ingested. If her husband was saying these words with such certainty, it could not prove otherwise. After all he was her protector, well-wisher and love incarnate. How could he do things prejudicial to her?

Now it was time for her to return. Her unannounced departure from the palace might give rise to myriads of rumors and tongue-wagging. Even the nasty king would prick his ears—what's happening? where's she gone and why? She could not take this risk. It might make people conclude that although the queen was in the know of her husband's location, she had kept the information to herself. And such a sentiment was going to taint her fair reputation. The royalty might be charged with playing a dubious game.

Now it was the time to depart. Releasing her gently from his parting embrace, the king bid her goodbye and wished her a happy return journey. Sachi left her better half with wistful eyes.

After bidding her goodbye, Indra felt unusually heavy at heart and concerned about her. How disturbed and shaken did she look! How long she must have suffered! At the palace, living under the perpetual terror of the debauch! How hard life must have been for her! In her troubled days she must have tried to share her fears and feelings of insecurity with someone but in whom could she confide? Living under the shade of constant terror is a terrifying experience. It rorbs one of the pleasures of life and saps the spirits. The more Indra thought of her harrowing times, the more disturbed was he. None of these could have happened to her, had he been there himself. It was actually he himself to blame. It was solely due to him that the pious, simple, good-natured lady had to suffer. He cursed himself for his indiscretion. He should not deserted his kingdom and run away like a coward. Like a strong man he should have been there itself and worked for his own regeneration. But no power in the universe can alter the way things have been planned by destiny. Therefore, whatever had happened was inevitable. Now the best course open to him was to cut short his sojourn in this corner of the world, and repair to his own kingdom at the earliest. As a caring and affectionate husband, he must do this to calm the lady's troubled mind.

Though Sachi had returned satisfied after her visit to her lord protector, certain anxieties and fears still lurked in her heart. Fear feeds on one's sense of insecurity and helplessness. Whatever her husband had advised her to do for getting out of the reign of terror, sounded so simple and natural, but suppose things don't turn up that way and there is a lapse somewhere. Then? She could not think anything beyond this. It looked so dark and uncertain. It was a sea of apprehensions.

But soon she changed her track of thinking. She shrugged off her the negative sentiments. She had heard that nothing comes out of nothing. Negative thoughts weaken us, sap our courage and immobilize our ability to think or act any good. They have a debilitating effect on the mind and discourage us from taking a bold step, as they speak only of defeat and destruction.

No, she must not give in to such self-destructive sentiments. It is not worth it. Has her meeting with her lord protector resulted in this! Won't it prove her undeserving and false to him, who loves her so passionately? Why should she ever doubt her ability to carry out the plan envisioned by him? He had reposed his faith in her capability: she must not disprove it. She must stand erect and prepare herself for the next meaningful move. She was sure to succeed. Doubting oneself nibbles away one's strength and makes one hollow from within.

6

Leaping for the Rainbow

KING NAHUSH WAS DISTRAUGHT. HE had not set his eyes on Sachi for quite some time, and was wondering where she had disappeared. Her absence stoked his desires for her. Granted, it had never been physical at all till now, but her very sight made hundreds of flowers bloom within him. She was like a whiff of the cool breeze in a dark, stuffy room.

———————————

Oh lo, she is here! But today's Sachi looked entirely different from what he had known and seen. Contrary to looking shrunken and withdrawn into herself, avoiding his amorous glances and meaningful looks, she looked quite inviting in her gorgeous robes and scintillating jewellery! Was it a ceremonial occasion? No, she did look so appealing and enchanting in the last few days. Her attitude and responses to him were different. His furtive glances were responded by her inviting eyes. Her body language too complemented it. She no longer looked cold and faraway. There was a definite thaw, a meltdown.

Perhaps it was the outcome of the persistent doggedness with which he had chased her. How long could she remain aloof and unaffected? After all she too was a human being, separated from her spouse for so many months. Won't she too be craving for the company of a man? It was natural. Who knows when and where will the hidden desires wake up and start stoking a person?

The other reason could be her realization of the fact that Indra would never return to the kingdom. No one knew how long he would be away and where he had gone. And because it was so, why not make friends with the incumbent ruler? Why to be inimical to him? He has been reasonably courteous and nice to us, often enquiring about our wellness. May be that my perception about him itself is skewed. He is essentially not a monster as my negative sentiments have made him to be. The poor chap has been living here, far away from his near and dear ones for our upkeep. Isn't it natural in these circumstances for him to seek the company of sympathetic souls? Time, outside his daily routine, must be hanging heavy on him. Man is after all a social creature, desirous of living with others. The fellow must be starved of human company. We must not be uncharitable and ruthless in our judgment of others, but give the due even to the Devil.

The supposed transformation in Sachi's conduct had given rise to similar diverse thoughts, all coloured favourably in the king's own favour. A prejudiced mind interprets things and events in its own favour. Even the immaterials appear to be concrete. To his fevered imagination, the queen seemed to be eager to approach him. But she was a woman after all. She had to be gracious and discreet in her silent communications. She could not afford to be vulgar and loud in articulating her desires. At such moments, women express themselves through symbols, glances and their body language. What more did he require? Hadn't she given sufficient signals till now? He should not be naive and stupid in the love game.

But the problem was how to go about it and make a proposal. It needed tremendous sensitivity. A stupid move was enough to ruin the show. The best was to visit her apartment as he had done several times in the past for the sake of enquiring about their wellness. It will make things look natural and formal.

"How are you, your highness?", he ventured, looking into her eyes. But he felt his eyes were also reflecting his suppressed desires.

"Thanks your honour. With you being here, what problems could we have? The whole kingdom feels itself blessed under your kind and affectionate rule", replied the queen with unbent eyes. This was very unusual. Up till now never had she looked straight into his eyes while replying. She had never stared into his face. Nahush felt emboldened. He could venture something more.

"Your highness, the nitty gritties of the administration don't permit time to call on your excellency. Sometimes loneliness is suffocating and one yearns for someone's company. But where to get one?" He looked meaningfully at her.

"Yes, your lord. You have well worded it. The demands of the throne are soul-killing, leaving no space for yourself. In such cases, it is but natural to seek the company of own people for unwinding oneself." Sachi was becoming increasingly straight forward, the king thought.

After the meeting the king was glad that he had been able to make a considerable dent in the erstwhile formidable fortress. Now the goal was just within an easy reach.

At the next meeting which followed soon after, things looked more cool and easy. There was none of the previous stiffness and aloofness. Time was proper now for the king to articulate his secret desires.

"Your highness, don't you ever feel as lonely as I do? I guess you too must be craving the company of someone to share your innermost thoughts."

"Yes, your excellency. We are all human beings given to similar feelings and sentiments. But there are decencies to be maintained and for that we have to suppress our real self.."

"Why not join the people in observing 'Vasantotsava' (the Spring festival) annually organized in the valley.? That will make the people happy. It will also help unwind ourselves."

"As you wish your highness" Sachi was glad to see that her tormentor was himself falling into the trap. Perhaps he was thinking that he was successful in finally winning over her, and together they would have a nice time. But for this she had to further stoke his fire.

To the fevered mind of Nahush, he was within an ace of victory. Not only had he there been a considerable transformation in the attitude of the 'fairy' of his imagination, she had also consented to be a partner in his 'adventure'. Its realization was just a matter of time, which was hardly round the corner. But they must thrash out the details and procedures of the meeting before hand. They were not ordinary people but those of the royal blood. Their movements will be watched by many eyes. They must not give a wrong signal for tongue-wagging. He knew that they needed utmost caution and discretion in moving forward. But it should not be too long. He had already waited impatiently for this momentous occasion. He felt he was bursting at seams with excitement.

The next meeting was a surprise one. It seemed even gods willed it. He had gone to the royal garden for a whiff of fresh air. It always soothed his troubled soul. He used to spend some time in a secluded grove surrounded by large trees. It was so heartening to see the flowers in bloom and trees laden with fruits. Suddenly a thought popped up from nowhere. Was not the fruition and flowering of trees the fulfillment of their wishes? Every tree here must have dreamt of being laden with flowers and fruit, and now they were having that. This is wish-fulfillment. When would his wishes be fulfilled? he wondered.. But here there was a difference. Whereas no force impeded the fulfillment of the desires of the trees, man's world abounded in such forces. He had to overcome several social hurdles to get what he wanted. But here the king's reverie received an unexpected jolt. There at the other end of the royal walk, he had noticed the queen alone. What a heaven-sent opportunity!! She must have come here for a change. There could not be any other reason. But how come that she too had come here almost at the same time as him! Gods certainly willed things in their favour and wanted them to unite. Wasn't it the right moment to finalise the programme of the meeting?

The queen was lost in enjoying the beauty of the hills, the lake, chirping of the birds, and gurgling of the stream. She never knew that Nahush had gingerly come very close to her. His welcome words took her by surprise. She reciprocated his greetings. It was the demand of courtesy. Now he needed both courage and decency in expressing his desire. A wrong stupid step, and the game would be spoilt.

"When did your highness come here?"

"I have been here for quite some time."

"But sorry, my eyes did not notice you."

"Your highness, this site always fascinates me and I come here quite often. Of all the beautiful places I have visited, this is the most enchanting and captivating. Standing here makes me lose the sense of time."

Nahush could not state otherwise. He too was a frequent visitor to this garden but that solitary grove attracted him more: it gave him peace and solace.

Now there was no time to lose. Such moments of closeness and privacy are not commonplace. Edging timorously towards her he said, "Your honor, I shall be blessed to have your company. I earnestly wish, it were the soonest. I should be glad to learn about the plan at the hill resort as suggested by you."

"Yes your honour, we have a royal resort amidst the groves, near the lake at the foot of the hill. It is so splendid and magnificent!"

Nahush was lost. His fevered brain was busy weaving unimagined fantasies around the place. How wonderful would it be there in her company! His amorous dreams were really coming to materialize. He woke up with a start from the current day dreaming. Her words were music to his hears.

"Yes, yes that's fine, madam. Your choice of the location is the most appropriate. But when are we expected to be there?", he could not withhold his query.

Curiously the queen did not look the least excited. It appeared as if she were saying things which are very normal and routine. Her words too did not show any emotion.

"Your honour, as you are aware, the annual festival of 'Vasantotsava" is only two days away. People will be celebrating the festival with the usual verve, excitement, loud music and dance for two days. During this period, people are carefree and freely move with their near and dear ones. During that celebration, I shall repair to the royal retreat towards the sundown. You may also make it by that time."

"All right, your highness." He was relieved that finally the meeting had been fixed. He would like to make the most of his time at the retreat..

"But your excellency, there is one condition for the meet."

"What's that, your excellency?" Nahush got jittery. What was it going to be? There is always some hurdle on the way.

"I wish you to come there by a palanquin, borne by the 'Saptarshis" (the seven great rishis) on their shoulders. Remember, you are a king, going to call on a queen. There must be something special about it. Any other mode of transport would have been inconsequential. You have to show how important you are. Even the revered sages are ready to carry your palanquin on their shoulders." the queen's face lighted with a meaningful smile.

Nahush's fantasy was further fired: it ran riot. At last he was going to throw his hands round the voluptuous queen and keep her in a tight embrace. How romantic and blissful the meeting would be!! Gods were certainly on his side. He had never dreamt that things would materialize the way he had dreamt. Rightly have the people said that once you wish to acquire an object and work assiduously towards its acquisition, you are sure to have it. Gods see that you get it. His dogged pursuit had ultimately borne fruits. But the way the queen had consented so easily, surprised him. She looked so formidable, withdrawn and cold earlier! How come she had mellowed!! May be she had her own compulsions. But why should all these be thought?

But her condition of arriving at the retreat in a palanquin, borne by sages, sounds rather stiff. Will the sages do so? Will it be proper? But why not? Weren't these the same people who had begged of me to come here from the Prithvilok? Don't they know my worth? They should certainly be doing this much favour to me, their king. Don't they owe me a favour? There could be some initial resistance on their part, but they will take it cool. If I have obliged them, isn't it their turn?

———————◆◆◆◆◆———————

The royal palanquin had arrived at the palace gate along with the venerated palanquin bearers in attendance. As soon as the king was intimated of the readiness of the transport, he scurried to the spot. He cast a glance around and looked satisfied with the arrangement. A flash of winning smile was noticed on his face, but the 'bearers' looked glum and serene. They reciprocated his smile with a wry one. Their countenance showed that the task assigned to them was lowly and demeaning, and they were doing it under duress. In his hurry and excitement to reach soon, he could not discern their looks and entered the palanquin.

Though the palanquin with its solitary passenger did not weigh much, for the unpractised bearers it was. It needed quite an effort to hoist it onto their shoulders and move forward. The very start was tardy and languorous, because the bearers needed to co-ordinate their steps with each other. They had never done it. Balancing the load on the shoulders was also problematic. As they moved on, they kept on shifting their load from one shoulder to the other. The tardy progress was annoying to the king. If they moved on at this rate, only heavens knew when he would be reaching the resort. The fantasies he had woven around the god-sent rendezevous, had made him restless. The faster would they carry him, the earlier would the queen be in his arms. Oh what a moment of bliss it would be!! It felt like the paradise coming at your feet.

But the speed of the bearers was pitiable. He urged them with lots of respect to hasten. For some steps it seemed to work, but soon it regained its tardy pace. He cajoled, then advised them and finally ordered them. But none of his words seemed to work.

Their slow progress was getting on his nerves. He feared that being late would spoil the game. The resort gate will be closed after a certain time as the queen had said. His delay might be construed as his unwillingness to keep the word, consequently compelling the queen to order the closure of the gate. That would be disastrous. He could not afford to miss this opportunity. But the things were not in his hands.

Finding that none of his urgings, requests and goadings had worked up till now, his irritation gave way to exasperation. He must teach a lesson to these time-wasters, albeit harsh. "What are you all doing, fools?Being stout and strong, you have willfully slowed your pace. Have you no sense of time and urgency? Come on, hurry up or you will be taken to task."

Enraged, the king forgot what he was doing and to whom. He kicked both of the front bearers on either side. The sacrilegious kicks worked as a bombshell. It had never occurred even in the wildest imagination that some one would kick the sages and treat them as slaves. Hadn't it been enough that they had agreed, even though reluctantly to carry his palanquin to some place?. And they were doing the job the best way they could. They were not manual labourers but belonged to the highest echelon of the society. They were venerated all around for their scholarship and spiritual achievements.

Angered at the dastardly act of the king, the tired and breathless sages revolted. Cursing him for his shameful demeanour, they said that such a person as he did not deserve to be their ruler. He was too mean and wicked to be one. Saying so they overturned the palanquin, out of which like a large ball he tumbled. They could watch him rushing toward the earth, with his hands raised in the air, crying for help.

After the return of the sages, the bizarre end of the royal journey had become the talk of the day. Now Sachi was able to realize the wisdom of her lord's counsel. She had little hope that the rascal's end would come so soon and she would be able to breathe in the free air only in a few days.

7

The Return of the Protector

IT WAS AFTER A LONG time that the people were seeing their king, their protector, at the throne. He looked verily rejuvenated—strong, tall, courageous and full of confidence. His long stint of meditation and penance had really transformed him. All the negative shades cast by the shameful rout at the hands of the asuras had vanished. People wished he had looked as impressive and powerful, as he was looking now for all times to come.

After acknowledging their hearty greetings and wishing them happier times in return, he enquired about the current state of affairs, people's problems and their solutions from his wise councillors. The problems posed by the attendees were mostly inconsequential and commonplace as usual.

But the next day's meeting was not formal, dealing only with public welfare and pleasantries. It was meant to discuss the core issue, i.e. their shameful defeat and the ways and means to retrieve the lost glory. It was proper to analyse the things threadbare and get the view of the assemblage. It was the question of their racial pride, their sullied image, and their self-respect as a nation. That's why Indra posed a question.

"Dear councillors, without mincing words, I wish to invite your considered views about our tragedy .. We, who had never tasted defeat ever since the world was created and always returned victorious from the fight, were humiliated this time. Please come forth with your views and suggestions without any fear or favour."

"My lord, our continuous victories in the past battles had made us complacent. We had grown conceited and always thought that the asuras were no match for us. Due to this feeling, we did not bother to re-evaluate ourselves and invent the latest in the technology of war.", said one.

"Yes my lord, we took every fight as a routine matter and underperformed every time, because we thought that victory ultimately would be ours.", said the second.

"My lord, once the result of a battle is known before hand, the fight becomes a mere exercise lacking in fervour and spirit."

Indra gracefully admitted the weaknesses. He too, like others had always taken such fights as a routine matter and dealt with it routinely." But this time our defeat was more because of another factor. Do you know that?" Indra wanted to find out their impression.

"Yes my lord, this time we noticed that while our brothers-in-arms were being killed and our number being reduced, the asuras' soldiers revived to life. This way, by virtue of a mysterious power they were never reduced in number. They always got new life after their death.".

"Yes I was referring to that. You have correctly observed the situation and found out the secret of their victory.", added Indra.

"My lord, we have learnt, albeit a rumor that Guru Shukracharya, the mentor of the asuras knows the art of reviving the dead. He possesses the science of Sanjeevni"

"Yes my lord, although the rumor sounds fantastic, but it has some truth. Otherwise how could the slain asuras be revived?"

"If they possess the secret of the revival of the dead, then they will never be defeated, because no body on their side would ever die. The feeling of immortality further strengthens their morale and makes them bolder."

"Then we are doomed for ever because in every fight they will have no loss of lives whereas we shall be the losers. O what a pity!"

"My lord, can't we too have that Sanjeevni? Only its acquisition will put us on an equal footing."

"My dear councillor, you have well said. But how can we have it? The secret of that science is known only to Shukracharya. And do you think he will share it with any one of us?" Indra's query was natural. Every army tries to possess a more potent and destructive weapon to have the better of the enemy. It never leaks out its description and potency. And as for this secret 'vidya' (knowledge), it is ridiculous to get it from the enemy camp."

The discussion cast a gloom on the assemblage. They could not make any headway. They seemed to have hit a blind alley. But in the mean time one of the younger members had a brainwave, "My lord, there is only one way. We could also learn about that secret 'vidya'."

Every pair of eyes was focused on the last speaker. How could any one learn about it? Who will part with the secret? Had the youngster gone off his head? Talking such nonsense!!

But the youngster was not to be cowed down. He came up with a suggestion.

"My lord, It's an extraordinary situation for us. And extraordinary decisions are taken in extraordinary times."

Some of the grey heads lost their patience and shot their query, "What do you want to say, young man? What extraordinary decisions are you talking about?"

"Venerable sirs, as you know Guru Shukracharya is the only person who knows the art and science of 'Sanjeevni'. We have to get it from him in whatever way we can."

"Young man, you think that the Guru will pass it on to any one? Don't be silly. Talk sense and don't befool your seniors.."

"No sirs, I am serious in what I say. And I have every hope it is practicable."

All eyes were curiously looking at him as if asking whether he had gone mad.

He continued, "My lord, as you know a real Guru deems it his sacred duty to impart knowledge to his disciple with all earnestness. He never discriminates between the knowledge seekers, because as our shastras say 'knowledge is no one's preserve. It must be passed on from the knower to the ignorant for its dissemination. The more the knowledge expands, the more lighted the world will be."

The grey heads saw nothing wrong in what the youngster had just said. "Yes young man, that's correct. But come to the point and tell us what you intend to."

"Honourable sirs, what I am going to say might appear to be far-fetched and bizarre but there is no harm in weighing it."

Every one's curiosity was roused..

"We have to think boldly and unconventionally. My humble suggestion is that one of our brightest youths goes to the ashram of Guru Shukracharya and learns the art and science of Sanjeevani at his feet. I am sure that pleased with the sincerity and devotion of the boy, he will part with the secret knowledge. But for that the student has to look serious and impeccable. The Guru has to be convinced that the 'vidya' would not fall into evil hands and would never be misused."

"Yes, that's a great idea. It's bold and meaningful. The Guru will certainly not refuse to pass on his knowledge to the disciple. But he will be alert and discreet. After all it's the question of his own survival and that of his adopted 'lok'. Young man, do you have anything more to add?"

"Yes, venerable sirs. With due humility I wish to further submit that our own Guru Brihaspati and Shukracharya are known to each other. They studied at the same ashram for a long time, and so far as I know they have tremendous mutual regards."

"Yes, yes, it's a fact. But what of this relationship!!"

"To my mind sirs, we should send such a young man to Shukracharya, who wins his confidence in his first meeting. And if this be done, then our purpose is served."

All were impressed with the practical wisdom of the young man. Every one wondered how such a novel idea had occurred to him.

"Yes my dear, what is your suggestion in this regard?"

"Veverable sirs, in my humble opinion, Kutch, the son of our Guru will be the most suitable candidate for this plan. He fits in the best. First of all he is the son of Shukrachrya's fast friend, and therefore nearer to his heart. So the boy will be easily accepted and be treated like his own son. To a disciple like this, the Guru will pass on his secret knowledge unhesitatingly, because he will be convinced of the worthiness of the disciple and the security of the knowledge."

It was certainly a wonderful idea, a clever plan to steal the secret 'vidya'. It would look so natural and simple on the surface but it would strike a gold mine. Certainly there was no other candidate as suitable as Kutch. But for that Guru Brihaspati's permission had to be obtained. After all, it was into the enemy land where the poor boy was going. Who could guarantee his safety and security in a strange land? His life would be at risk every waking moment. Being a resident of 'devlok', he might be treated as an enemy agent and might even be killed. Any fear that he had gone there to learn the secret 'vidya' was enough for the asuras to eliminate him. Was it proper to push a lamb into a lion's den? The helpless creature could never survive in the den. Similarly, Kutch's survival in that hostile atmosphere would be at the mercy and whims of the enemies.

Granted that Guru Shukracharya would provide him a protective shield, but how long could he do it? He would himself be at the risk of being touted as an enemy sympathizer. No, the risks were many. There was no ray of hope.

And Guru Brihaspati too had to be prevailed upon. Would he willingly permit his son to be dispatched to the enemy country? And for what? Who will guarantee his well being? It was a million dollar question. Even lord Indra had to think twice before prevailing upon the Guru. Was it not too selfish? Why should the Guru sacrifice his only son for the masses? Why only he, and not others? But they all said that Kutch was different from any other candidate due to his relationship with Guru Brihaspati, who in turn was the friend of that Guru. So only he qualified for the plan. Guru Shukracharya may not accept any other boy as his disciple. For the son of his friend he might have a different feeling. He would inspire his confidence naturally.

Any way, Guru Brihaspati was ultimately prevailed upon and Kutch was sent to the ashram of Guru Shukracharya.

⬥⬥⬦⬥⬥

8

A Stranger at the Door

KUTCH DID NOT KNOW WHAT to do. His two timorous knocks at the cottage door, had yielded no response. Every where around the cottage prevailed an eerie silence. There were a few cottages in the neighbourhood, but separated from each other with large stretches. Flowering and fruit trees of all varieties were swaying in the gentle breeze. He could also see a few cows and their calves in the nearby shed, and some deer fawns gamboling about in the open courtyard. He was sure that guided by others, he had come to the right cottage. His young heart was growing impatient. He gave another knock at the door. Some one opened it gingerly. A girl with slightly disheveled hair in a careless attire, stood in the door frame. Both looked at each other with deep amazement. Meanwhile a man's voice enquired from within, "Devi dear, who is there?" Devyani was still looking at the visitor with rapt attention. What a human form! what large eyes! What a beautiful nose on the face, surrounded by curls!Was he not the kind of man she had seen in her dreams? How come that he is here! Getting no reply from his daughter, the man was coming there himself. She could hear the clattering of his wooden slippers.

His second call woke her up from her reverie. She could not reply. What will dear father say? "Revered father, there is some one at the door", she uttered brokenly, as her father neared.

Seeing the Guru standing before him, Kutch stepped forward and falling flat on the ground touched his feet with his hands and the head. The old man expected him to rise soon but he lay in that state for quite a few moments. The Guru then lifted him up and looking into his eyes said, "Who are you, my son?"

"Gurudeva, I am Kutch, the son of your friend Brihaspati."

"O God, son of Brihaspati!! son of Brihaspati!! He was such a dear friend just like my brother. How is he?", saying so he drew him to his hairy chest for a warm embrace.

"He is fine, sir. He has sent his sincere regards to you. He often remembers his ashram life, his teachers, his friends—specially you.."

The Guru was excited beyond words. It was such a pleasure to see the son of his long-forgotten friend. The boy looked so handsome, so well-bred and so cultured.

"What brings you here, my son?"

"Honourable sir, my father has sent me to study at your blessed feet. He thinks that your ashram is the only place where I could get the best education. In his considered opinion, there is none in the world who could be as competent as you for my education." His words slightly flattered the Guru. But he was mighty impressed with the way the boy had conducted and articulated himself.

All this while Devyani stood there transfixed as a mute spectator to the pleasant spectacle. It was exciting to learn that Kutch had come here to study under her father and stay. It would be a long stay. The very thought seemed to be fulfilling her dream. It was difficult to explain why she was so pleased with the way things were happening.

Turning to Devyani, the Guru said, "Devi dear, you have already learnt who this boy is. From today onwards, he would be a member of our household and would stay put until his course is complete. Like me, he too would be your liability for all his daily requirements. And Kutch would also contribute in whatever way he can, in running the household.

The Guru's words were accepted by both. With one stroke he had both welcomed and adopted the young boy.

⎯⎯⎯◈◆◈◆◈⎯⎯⎯

The boy had come as a fresh breeze in the humdrum existence of the ashram. Life up till now had felt so monotonous and inane, consisting only of the Guru's meditation, 'sandhya', puja, teaching the wards and passing occasional instructions to his daughter pertaining the household. He earnestly wished he had been blessed with a son like his friend Brihaspati was. Any way, for unknown reasons to him, Kutch appeared to be his own son. How nice, if this boy had stayed here for ever as a companion of Devyani. But soon he reprimanded himself for mixing up two diverse images—the boy as a son and then as his son-in-law. At the root of this day dreaming was his desire to be related to him in any fashion.

Had the Brahmani (mother of Devyani) been alive, she might have borne him such a gem. But alas!, that was not to be. She had left for the other 'lok' years ago, leaving the angel-like child to him to rear. Only he knew how hard life had been since then, tending the little girl. Women are more competent than their male counterparts in this regard. However, by his good luck, the child had grown into a girl of rare charm and grace. His neighbours and colleagues often praised her for her beauty and unearthly charm. But their remarks seemed to have gone into her young head and made her slightly haughty and conceited. Being the apple of the eyes of her indulgent father, she ruled the house. The Guru would leave no stone unturned in carrying out her wishes, however bizarre and difficult they were. Actually he had no other alternative. He wanted to keep her happy at every cost. Who else did he have as his own in the family? He could not afford to displease her for fear of her tantrums. His excessive leniency to her had therefore, spoilt her. As she had never heard a 'No' from him for anything in life, she tended to believe that she could have anything in the world.

Her father would move heaven and earth to ensure that her desires were fulfilled.

But sometimes he was subjected to a feeling of sadness for her. As a man he would often go out and meet other spiritual practitioners and neighbours, but the poor child had to remain within the four walls of the ashram. She was kept busy with the domestic chores and had therefore, little chance of meeting her girl friends in the ashram complex. Mostly she was left to herself with no one to talk to or share her feelings. For that she would have to make an effort. But now that this boy had come, she would be a happier person. And fortunately, all this was happening. He could notice her now chirping and twittering like a bird, moving here and there with remarkable alacrity. She had no time to look irritable and unhappy. Her pleasant disposition had eased his life too. No longer did he have to find the cause of her displeasure and make efforts to bring smile on her face.

9

Like a Fish Taking to Water

TIMES HAD SUDDENLY CHANGED FOR Guru Shukracharya. After God knows how many years, he was feeling relaxed and had more time to himself. The sudden turning of the tables made him think of the times of discomfort and suffering. Man tends to compare his present with the past if the days be different, as it creates a sense of satisfaction and achievement.

He vividly remembered his last day at the Gurukul where after years of learning shastras and 'guruseva'(service to the guru) he had completed his education. Now like every other intern he was free like a bird to find his mooring. The 'vidyarthis' (students) coming out of the ashram would first of all try to find an employment, either in a royal court or with an aristocrat: sometimes as a king's advisor or a tutor to the kids of the aristocrat. Bur every one was not so lucky as to get such opportunity. He remembered how for quite a few years, he wandered from place to place in search of patronage but ill luck seemed to dog him everywhere. Meanwhile his problems had multiplied because of marrying a girl for setting a house. He could not lead a vagabond's life indefinitely. So now it was the question of the sustenance of two.

Like dozens of his classmates who had been equally unlucky, he started his own ashram in the woods on the outskirts of the capital city. Being a suitable location, he soon got students from the city and the neighbourhood. After all the kids of the government servants, business men, aristocrats and such high ups had to be educated, and who else other than the trained teachers like him could do it?

With the passage of time, the flow of students increased and those coming there from faraway places, begged of the Guru to let them stay with him in the ashram premises. Such prayers were not uncommon those days. The Guru had to sympathetically consider their case and arrange for them accordingly. Weren't the outsiders entitled to the quality education as much as the locals? This system was called the 'gurukula'(teacher's extended family or household). The students were not only imparted lessons in various branches of knowledge, they were also made to have practical experience of life. They would go to the forest for collecting firewood for the kitchen, tend the cows and the calves, milk them and take them to the field for grazing. Some of them were made to look after the agricultural sector, as it was here that their food was grown. None of the students or their parents ever grudged it, because the training in the gurukul catered not only to that of the mind but the body too. In the end, it prepared the students for life itself, as after graduating from here, they had to start their life on their own.

Guru Shukracharya carried on with the practice of gurukula only for some years. His reputation as a brilliant teacher travel;ed beyond the boundaries of the hermitage on to the capital. One day Brishparva, the Asur king, invited him to his court. The king urgently needed some one as a mentor and as an advisor, because the previous incumbent was unable to discharge his duties due old age and ill health. The Guru accepted his offer but declined to stay on the palace premises. He felt that life in the ashram was more compatible with his life style. Though living away, he would always be available to the court. The king would send for him any time he liked. He would make to the court the soonest possible.

The king was mighty impressed with the simplicity of the guru, as very few souls decline the offer of an ostentatious living. His regards for the sage multiplied. The only thing that did not worry the king was his ashram was only at a few minutes' distance. He could be contacted without any loss of time.

⟺◆◆◈◆◆⟺

By virtue of his sincerity and diligence, Kutch had greatly endeared both to the Guru and his daughter. He did not hesitate in performing even the unpleasant-looking domestic chores like cutting down the dry trees and making smaller pieces out of them for storage, for use in the rainy season and winter. He would tend the cows, calves and the oxen. Sometimes he would even work as a helping hand to Devi in the kitchen. After the morning 'swadhyaya' (learning the lesson), he would carry the milk animals to the pasture and return with them late afternoon. Sometimes it seemed as if the boy had been an intrinsic part of this family: he had always been there. Being an outsider, he had adjusted himself so smoothly.

Initially Kutch felt slightly uncomfortable, dealing with the naughty girl. His initial relationship could be termed as one of indifference, but gradually both had gelled and seemed to be enjoying each other's company. The Guru's occasional absence from the ashram (he often went to the king's court) gave the girl opportunities to play innocent pranks on the reticent Kutch and tease him to react. His characteristic unresponsiveness further whetted her appetite to irritate him, but he would remain calm.

In course of time these childish sentiments gave way to fondness for each other. It would be wrong to attribute the same feeling to each other in equal measure. Devi had started adoring and weaving dreams around the youth. She would often decorate herself with garlands and flowery ornaments in her hair and ears. Looking at the mirror in such an outfit, gave her an indescribable joy. She looked so pretty and bewitching! Who won't be attracted towards such a charming figure? After assessing herself in the mirror, she would present herself before Kutch and asked how she looked. Busy with his books, he would invariably give her a passing look and mumble something, meaning it was o.k. This would offend her ego. She had come here with such huge expectations of hearing paens from him, but he was such a boring soul. No sense of appreciation of her beauty! She had thought that he would look admirably into her face, her large kohl-lined eyes, her heaving chest, and her growing bosom, down to her feet. But he had thoroughly disappointed her. She wished she had thrown away his books and writing materials out of the room, but she reigned herself. Was she not disturbing him in his studies? Wasn't he completing his assignment as directed by the guru? Won't he reprimand him for being irresponsible? This steadied her and she realized her folly……………….

Kutch was not as insensitive and unappreciative as Devi had taken him to be. He was aware of her feminine charms, her childishness, and her annoyance with him for being unresponsive. But he always remembered the words of caution made by his father. He was asked to remember why he had been selected and why he was sent to the ashram. His focus ought to be on achieving what had been planned. As only on that depended the survival of the future generations of devas. He had come here with a purpose: a sacred mission. He should not fritter away his energies by falling into the trap of this charming girl. Falling in love would bode ill for devas. If they were intensely in love with each other, the asuras would like them to settle in their own 'lok'. That would be cheating the people who had sent him with high hopes. He had therefore, to sacrifice his personal likes and dislikes and work assiduously for his people.

It was Mahashivratri—the night of Lord Shiva, the greatest god of the asuras. Shiva was revered and worshipped in the other lokas too, but for the asuras he was the only god whom they revered and worshipped with tremendous fervour. On this day all the asuras would fast, prepare garlands of marigold, collect 'bilva patra' (leaves of bel tree), and visit the temple of the Lord. But in addition to visiting the temple, every house worshipped Him at its own place.

Both Guru Shukracharya and Kutch left for the 'Padma sarovar' (the lotus pond) for their ablution much before the dawn. Devi too would be going there but she would do it after them. Therefore, after their departure, she hurriedly finished the domestic chores and left for the pond. When she came, she found not many souls bathing there. Some men were bathing in the pond, and women folk were waiting for them to finish. Along with some of them, she waited for her turn behind a clump of trees. Her eyes were eagerly looking for Kutch. Oh where was he! Soon she noticed the well-built, muscular Kutch emerging out of the water, with water dripping from his long curly hair, his ear lobes, the broad chest, and the wet dhoti sticking to his muscular legs. The rays of the rising sun, added to his magnificent figure. It seemed Indra himself was coming out of the water. Devi was mesmerized by his handsome figure. It resembled the prince of her frequent dreams. She felt like rushing and clinging to the grand figure.

Earlier too she had been here for bath on the occasion of this festival, but it was for the first time that she was seeing him in such a magnificent form. She deemed herself blessed that she was staying under the same roof with such a handsome person. The phantom of Kutch haunted her for the whole day. She wanted to express her admiration for him at a proper time………………..

Plenty of flowers had been collected for preparing garlands for the puja and loose offerings both at home and the temple. Pujas at both the places consumed most parts of the day. It was a day for reciting mantras, singing prayers, devotional songs dedicated to the Lord to the accompaniment of drums, conchs and cymbals. The whole air rang with loud merriment. As it was the middle of Vasant (spring season), people applied dry colours to each other and also threw the dust into the air above. There was universal joy and bonhomie. Nobody grudged if he/she was liberally smeared with the dry colour. Even the familiar faces were becoming unrecognizable due to the heavy smear of diverse colours.

They had all gone to the temple together, but had to wait long due to the heavy rush of the worshippers. While returning, the Guru could not accompany them. He had met some court officials in the vast temple courtyard. Even on such a day of festivity, they were discussing administrative matters. Kutch and Devyani headed home. She was thrilled to be walking in his company and wanted to talk, but her queries were replied in a few measured words. Like other girls of the neighbourhood, she too had liberally used fragrant flowers of different hues for self-embellishment. She was wearing necklace, garlands, armlets and bangles on her body. Some flowers were also pinned to the hair. She was excited with joy. She wished Kutch had expressed his admiration for her, as she had done to him. As soon as they entered the ashram and Kutch made for his room, she followed him tip-toeing. She was carrying a garland in her hands. Before he could turn around, she appeared like a lightning and put the garland round his neck. He was both amused and surprised. What's she doing! He could notice a mischievous twinkle in her eyes. Before he could compose himself, she had also pinched his cheeks with her fingers.

"What's this Devi, a garland round my neck!"

"Yes, so what? All of us are putting it today. It is the Lord's 'prasad' and we sport it. I put one round your neck because your chest looked so bare without it."

"Aha, I see, yes, I did not put on one like that because I deemed it unnecessary."

"It's not unnecessary, dear. It is customary."

"But do you realise the significance of a garland put by a girl round a young man's neck?"

"No, no please tell me that significance."

"My dear Devi, it means "Swayamvar" i.e. selecting your life partner. Garlanding is a sort of seal on the relationasip."

"Oh I see, I should not have offended you. I never meant it. You think you are the best person for me as my spouse? No, no, dear, there are pretty many in the world", she said with naughty playfulness. But she realized she might have hurt his feelings. By saying that there were many more handsome than him, was she not denigrating him? 0 God, what a blunder she had committed! Could she get a better partner for herself than him? Someone has said that many a true word is spoken in jest. But she certainly did not mean it. Granted that she never meant it, but what if he had taken the remarks to his heart? Wasn't a handsome young man being rebuffed by a maid? She cursed herself for the blunder. Someone has said that words are like arrows: once shot, they never come back but hit the target. Alas, she should not have been so rash and unscrupulous! Overcome by guilt and fear of losing the prince of her dreams, she got desperate. She had to make amends immediately or it might be too late.

She tried to look into his eyes. Was he hurt and displeased? But his face looked as serene and unmoved as ever. It rarely reflected his inner thoughts. Without knowing what she was doing, she held both of his palms into hers and peering into his eyes, said, "Dear friend, are you sore? Displeased with me for my careless words?"

Kutch was not ready for this scene: she holding his hands in hers. From his eyes it appeared that her words had

63

not at all bothered him. He knew her temperament: childish, frivolous and playful with a crystal heart. "No dear, Devi, I'm not at all upset. Actually I didn't hear your words. And I know that you can't be rough and indecent. Shouldn't I ignore the careless remarks?"

His words were soothing. They had set her anxieties to rest. Now she could feel light at heart. Kutch was too simple at heart. He could not misconstrue other's careless words but took them superficially. It's the speaker's intention and the total personality which matters when he makes a statement.

She detached her nervous palms from his and left for her room.

———————❖◄❖►❖———————

10

The Conjecture

THE ARRIVAL AND PRESENCE OF Kutch at the Guru's ashram was gradually noticed by all and sundry. They were curious to know who he was and why he had come. He was certainly not a guest or a visitor who returns after a brief stay. He seemed to have been adopted and naturalized by the Guru's family. All sorts of wild guess and conjecture gave rise to tongue-wagging. It was certain that the lad was known to the Guru very intimately. Might be he was his nephew or a friend's son. But why should he be here for so long? Things had to be checked and confirmed. But who would ask the Guru? It was no body's business to question who had come to the ashram and how long would he stay. It was completely his private affair. How did it concern others? But you can't stop the idle talkers and tale-carriers. It was anyway decided that some one from the common folk would check up the facts with the lad himself when alone. And they got a chance.

One day while Kutch was herding his Guru's milch cows and calves, he was met by a middle-aged man on the way.

"Well my boy, pardon me for interrupting you." Kutch was both amused and surprised. What did the stranger want to ask him? He looked questioningly at the man.

"No sir, it's all right." replied Kutch with due courtesy.

"What's your name?"

"Kutch."

"New in this campus?"

"Yes sir."

"Where do you live?"

"At the ashram of Guru Shukracharya."

"No, no, I meant your original dwelling place. This place is not your permanent home."

"I see. I belong to 'swarga', the world ruled over by Lord Indra."

"Oh yes, then how come that you are here? from 'swarga' lok to 'asur' lok?"

"For me it's not at all different, sir. Life everywhere is the same. The same cosmic power supervises everywhere."

The questioner was impressed with the way the lad had conducted himself and answered his queries. Didn't appear to be suppressing facts."

The information gathered from the boy was passed on to the curious lot. But more was needed. Why should he be here? Who had ever heard of a soul coming form the land of gods to the land of demons? They are so different culturally and civilizationally. No, no, there is something more than meets the eyes. There must be a secret purpose for his visit. He must have been sent here with a mission. More about this could be gathered at the next meeting.

Kutch was met again by the same soul on the next day at the same place. Kutch got curious. Why was this man after him?

"Well my dear son, whose son are you?"

Kutch looked rather intently at the questioner. Why was he after having his details? He thought of skirting his query under some excuse but that might make the matter worse. He would be buying the general displeasure and ill will of the populace. He softened. There was nothing wrong in answering, but he needed to be wary.

"I am the son of Guru Brihaspati, sir."

"Ah Guru Brihaspati! Who doesn't know your honourable father, my son? He is well known for the depth of his learning and wisdom. There is none in the universe to match his pedantry."

The boy looked pleased. His father was being eulogized by some one in a foreign land. It sounded music to his ears. He was proud of him.

"Then how come that you are here, my son? Does your father know that you are here?"

"Yes he knows. I have come here for studying at the feet of Guru Shukracharya."

"Why should the son of such a learned and renowned father come all the way to the 'asur lok' to study at the feet of our Guru who is not as illustrious as your father!"

"No sir, you don't know the significance and value of your Guru. My father knows it."

"How is it? Have they ever met?"

"Yes, both of them were classmates at the same 'guru kul' and have stayed together for several years. That period was enough to have a mutual understanding."

"Yes I see, son. But son, it doesn't satisfy me. If both were the disciples of the same Guru, they must be equally qualified."

"You are right, sir. Still there are individual differences. Only they are aware of their mutual strengths and weaknesses. No father would like his son to imbibe his own shortcomings. He would guard against it and try to see that his son blooms into a perfect person."

"Kutch's words left nothing more to enquire. What more could be sought? But cynics amongst the populace had their own suspicion. They smelt a sinister plan of the crafty devas in sending the boy here. They were past masters at the game of deceit and other mind games.

11

The Final Solution

TO THIS LOT OF THE self-appointed extreme patriots, things were not as simple as they appeared superficially. And in actual fact they had been planned to appear innocuous to avoid any suspicion.

It was their third meeting today. They had gathered to discuss the shape of the things to come, in view of the strange happenings.

"I'm afraid, we are heading for very bad days," said the oldest.

"Why so worried and disturbed, sir?"

"My fellow men, I am apprehending the end of our race. You may not be able to foresee that, but I can do."

"What's that, sir?"

"The wily gods have dispatched their spy."

"Which spy, sir?"

"Oh that boy. He is their spy. In the garb of studying at the feet of our Guru, he is here to steal the 'vidya' of Sanjeevni."

"No sir, it is improper to impute evil motives without sufficient ground. How can that simple lad be a spy?"

"Can't an outside student come to our Guru for learning at his feet? We are not aware of the importance of our own Guru, but others know his depth. Being unlettered and uneducated, how can we know his worth?"

"We ought to be proud of the fact that our Guru's fame has spread so far and wide that even the Guru of the devas has sent his son to study under him."

Most of the souls supported this line of argument and heavily discounted the baseless fears of the grey head. He was therefore, exasperated, and said to himself, "These fools are not able to look into the future." and then he said in public," Friends, I'm not disputing the greatness of our revered Guru. He is certainly a gem, a great soul. Any well-meaning father would like to get his son educated at the feet of such a renowned scholar.

But that's not the point. My fears are based on his simplicity and child-like temperament."

"Yes, he is such a man. These are the attributes of a 'mahapurush" (a great soul). He treats every one with tremendous equanimity. And what's wrong with it? The boy, as learnt, in none else than the son of his own class mate."

The listeners had a reason to be astonished. "Was Guru Brihaspati, a class mate of our Guru?"

"Yes my dear friends, he was."

"Honourable sir, then there should be no reason for anxiety. He is a familiar figure, and not a total stranger. It will be a pleasure for a Guru to teach his own friend's son.

"My dear fellow men, I am really saddened by your inability to see the things in the distance. Your thinking is so much coloured by the superficial glare. You are too eager to simplify things and not care to look at their bottom. Such a folly is reprehensible and will ruin us."

They got alerted. Why was the grey head continuously discounting their opinion? What actually made him that different? Why is it that he was still resisting and not coming round to our view? For that, he must be having solid reasons. Sometimes a majority is wrong and ill-informed, and those in one or two are right, because they have dared to think differently. Actually they are the ones who caution a crowd against the pitfalls lying ahead on their path. They are the real salt of the earth. No, no, they should listen to him. People must know the grounds of their apprehensions.

"All right, sir. we are sorry for not sharing your views up till now. In a healthy society every one is entitled to his opinion and we must give it due regard. We shall be glad to hear your view."

Gauging their curiosity, the senior said, "Have you thought of the reason why a man like Guru Brihaspati himself should send his son to our land, when he is himself capable of teaching him well?"

There was an air of general disbelief. They all looked at him with questions in their eyes.

"The reason is simple. Devas know that we have defeated them only by virtue of our Guru's knowledge of Sanjeevani. As long as that knowledge stays with us, we shall never lose the battle against them. Rather they will be the losers. And it hurts their pride. The thought of losing all the future battles can't be digested. How miserable they must be! That's why to kill the matter for ever, the crafty devas have planned to steal that knowledge from us. They must have consulted Guru Brihaspati for neutralizing our strength.. Being aware of his relations with our Guru, they must have prevailed upon him to agree to send his son in the garb of studying and ultimately getting that 'vidya'."

There seemed to be a general consensus. May be that the old man is correct. They again looked at him for more of such information.

"Brihaspati knows how child-like and simple his friend is. He will have no hesitation in passing on his knowledge to his disciple, because it is said that a true guru is he, who replicates himself in the form of another man. He feels proud that he has recreated his duplicate and the knowledge reposed with him till now, will not die with him. Knowledge must be passed on and not be allowed to stagnate."

And then imagine. If the 'vidya' of sanjeevani goes to our enemies what will happen of us? It would be disastrous because devas would have capitalized on it and we shall never be able to defeat them again. And that will be our end." He looked questioningly into the eyes of of his listeners.

It created a sense of despair in the assemblage. As per the speaker, their disaster was just round the corner. Their fate seemed to be sealed. The crooked devas had really played a nasty game upon them. Where's the guarantee that the Guru would be discreet enough to set aside the 'vidya', and not pass it on to the spy?"

"Honourable sir, what you apprehend might one day become a reality. And as you said, that will be the end of all of us. We had lost all the previous battles against the devas up till now, but defeated them only by virtue of the secret 'vidya' of our guru. For our survival we have to see that the nasty game of devas doesn't succeed."

"But how can that be, sir? Shall we inform our king of this nefarious game with a request to stop the guru from passing on the knowledge to his disciple?"

"No dear friends, it won't work. Our king is so overwhelmed with the knowledge and the spartan life style of our guru that he won't muster up courage to say so. Moreover, he might be of the opinion that the guru was wise enough to discriminate between what is right and what is wrong, what is proper and what is improper."

"Honourable sir, you are right. It is beyond our king to do so. Then what to do to preempt it? It is a question not only of our own survival but that of the coming generations of the asuras."

"I am glad friends, that you are able to visualize the catastrophe that might befall us."

"Yes sir, we are really terrified at the thoughts of the coming days. But what should we do?"

"Brothers, please don't leave everything to me. You too are blessed with the power of reasoning and deciding a matter. Think of a solution."

A frantic discussion ensued.

"We can't stop the guru from teaching his disciples."

"We can't stop the king from doing the worst"

"We can't stop either. If neither is possible, then the inevitable will happen. Nobody can stop it and then let's be prepared for the worst. If we are incapable of saving ourselves, we have to be ready for mass destruction."

The short remarks of the speakers reflected the general despondency and helplessness. They seemed to have hit a blind wall. No other alternative was in sight. In the mean time some one burst out with these words:

"Honourable sir, if neither of these is possible, then there is only one thing that is possible."

All eyes were focused on him. What was he going to say?

"Sir, the only option left is to stop the spy from getting the 'vidya' from the guru."

"But how can we do that? No one can stop a disciple from hearing his teacher."

"The answer is that if there is no one to learn, whom will the guru teach?"

All wondered at this sentence. What is meant by "no one to learn?"

"My hint is clear. Let's finish off the spy and that will be an end to all our woes."

There was a silence for a while. "Isn't it cruel?How can we kill a boy who is our guest! It's a heinous crime and totally unethical. How can we kill a boy who has come to learn merely on the basis of a conjecture? Learning is such a sacred thing. No, no, it's totally against the morals."

"Well friends, it's immoral and unethical, I agree. But in case of an emergency even the most drastic step is desirable. One little wrong is preferable to the mass annihilation. It can be condoned. Let's not be carried away by the meaningless customs and ethics. Who will follow these customs if we cease to exist as a race? I strongly believe that one life is nothing in the face of the mass survival."

People seemed to be convinced. Though the act being proposed was extremely wicked and savage, it was desirable in the face of the problems that were to follow.

So the die was finally cast. Its execution was left for some to decide.

12

The Dastardly Game Plan

THE PLAN TO ELIMINATE THE unprepared and unarmed boy was very simple. The marauders did not want that their victim should smell the plan. They would chase him wherever he goes without being noticed and ambush him at the appropriate moment. The final act will be committed at a place where no one cares to go. Armed with arrows, swords and axe, they will fan in different directions, hiding behind bushes or trees. And once a typical bird call is sounded, they will pounce on the quarry and finish him off immediately. It was decided not to leave his slain body in the open but to hack into pieces and feed them to the hungry wolves.

The plan sounded so vicious and inhuman but this sordid decision was reached on purpose. They believed that when the guru would not be able to find the boy returning home after grazing the cows, he would naturally be worried as to what had happened and why had he not returned. Being his friend's son, he was morally responsible for his safety and security. He was the boy's local guardian. And should any harm befall the boy, he would be held accountable. What reply could he give to his friend then? And would the people say? And if the sage found his slain body, then by virtue of the power of Sanjeevani, he would revive him. His revival would present the same problem again before us. It was as good as not decimating him then. But if his body parts were fed to the wolves, there was no hope of his regeneration. And that would be the end of the story.

Devyani had a great weakness for the red lotus. There were white and blue varieties in the nearby pond, but the red variety bloomed only in the jungle lake. One could see them there—some in full bloom, some half and some just sprouting into buds. Half bloomed and the budding ones were ideal for preparing personal ornaments—like bracelets, bangles, necklace and ear rings. Once adorned, they heightened the beauty of the wearer. And as for Devyani, it suited her the best: turning her into a bewitching fairy. She had an irresistible desire to wear them and watch her reflection in the mirror. What to say of the members of the other sex, she would herself fall for the figure in the mirror. And it was also important, because Kutch had been charmed by her looks on the Mahashivratri day. On that day she was wearing such beautifying aids. But how to get them? Her father was too occupied with the court affairs and his own spiritual practices to attend to her petty needs. The presence of Kutch had greatly relieved him because he was there to look into such affairs.

"Kutch dear, will you mind doing me a favour?" Kutch heard while moving out with the cattle.

"What's that, Devyani? Want me to bring something, manage something?"

"Yes, my demands are very ordinary. I greatly desire to have some red lotuses in their different stages of blooming. You know, such ones are there in the jugle lake."

"There is nothing to worry about. Please wait till my return. To day I might be back a little earlier. Flowers will be useful only then."

Devyani was excited at his words: thinking of the plan of self-embellishment as well as surprising Kutch by that.

13

Hunting The Quarry

THE MARAUDERS NOTICED KUTCH AT the expected time. He came to the open grass land and supervised the animals for a while. This was not the right time for attack. Because being open on all sides, he might notice them coming towards him. And sensing some trouble, he might run away or cry for help. That would foil their game. It was proper to wait and follow his activities.

Good luck seemed to be on their side. From their hiding places they noticed him supervising the cattle while sitting on a little mound. He stayed there for about an hour, then moved towards the depth of the jungle. The lake was some distance away. Whistling in the woods, he was seeing proceeding further. This was the right moment. There were hundreds of tall and shady trees all around in addition to shrubs and creepers. Though it was sunny outside, but the sun did not visit this dark area. Suddenly there was a bird's familiar call. At this sprang out the assailants from different corners. First of all they shot an arrow. Why go near? As soon as he fell down and fainted because of the poisonede dart, they surrounded him. Their quarry lay before them—immobile and limp. They looked at each other meaningfully as if asking about the next move. But it had already been decided. No mercy had to be shown to the enemy agent. Soon the body was hacked into smaller pieces with swords and axes. Smelling blood, the prowling wolves were attracted. They were lucky that they did not have to hunt for their food, and were getting small pieces of flesh and bone for nothing. It was all a cake walk.

After being sure that no body part was left behind, and nothing of the boy remained, the assailants felt satisfied. They had done a great service to their land and to their coming generations. The whole asura race would be grateful to them for their invaluable contribution. They deserved to be publicly commended for this.

After the cows and calves had finished grazing, they were looking for their guide as usual. But he was nowhere to be seen. They lowed and mooed, as if calling for him, but there was no response. They thought he might have returned earlier today. Waiting for a few minutes, they followed their path back home.

At home Guru Shukracharya was preparing himself for the evening prayers after the usual ablution. He noticed the animals return without the boy. Where was he? These creatures were always escorted by him. Where had he gone!! May be that Devi had sent him on some special errand. But in that case he would have performed the job during the grazing time of the animals and returned with them. Why not ask Devyani herself? She might say something about it.

"Devi," he gave her a call. She was inside the room. She came rushing. Perhaps her father needed something. "Why is it that Kutch hasn't come along with the animals? Did you send him on an errand?"

"Yes father, I had requested him to bring some lotus flowers from the jungle lake. It wasn't much of a task. He should have been back along with them."

"Yes dear, it should have been like that, but it is not so. Where could he possibly go? Drowned in the lake? No, he is a good swimmer. The flowers there are within an easy reach. He can't be lost in the forest either. He is well aware of its inside. He is not a stranger to that area."

The boy's disappearance was a matter of real concern for the guru. If the boy has been harmed, he would be responsible for it. He would be blamed for being indifferent and callous. It might be even said that he did not care for the boy, because he was not his own child. The greater worry was the lot of his friend in 'Sawrgalok'. What will he say that he had sent his only son to his friend, thinking that he would take affectionate care of him and see that no harm is done to him. Seeing her father's anxious face, the girl too got panicky. What had happened to the prince of her dreams? To the world she had woven around him?

Suddenly she was reminded of the wild rumor, one of her childhood friends in the ashram complex had breathed? "Devi dear, the asuras suspect your friend Kutch, of being the spy of devas. They say that he has come here from 'swarga' on a secret mission. The asuras would not let it happen. If needed, they would not hesitate even in killing him." But Devyani had rubbished the rumor. What nonsense was Gayatri talking about? She often carried such wild tales. She had nothing better to do, as Devi often remarked. But it seemed, her apprehensions were well-founded. The thought of his tragic end seemed to have shattered her.

Her eyes watered. She couldn't help herself crying. How could she live without him? He had become such an intrinsic part of her existence.

"Dear father, kindly do something to find him out. Bring him here. I cannot live without him. I love him. He is my life." Devyani was sobbing inconsolably. The guru's heart seemed to break. He was faced with a double tragedy. Devyani was his only beloved child. He could not think of living without her. And now she says she cannot live without the boy. The boy too was his weakness and liability. He was perturbed and was at his wit's end. If the boy was not found, he would lose the girl too. He would have gone to the forest with a flame torch, but it would not serve the purpose because of the wind blowing in the open grass land.

Seeing her father himself jittery and deeply troubled, she got hysterical. Her father would not have felt so disturbed and desperate, had the things been under control. It definitely meant that an evil had befallen Kutch, and he had been eliminated by the hired criminals. She was helpless, distraught and in intense grief.

She fell at his feet and looking into his sorrowful eyes she begged, "Dear father, do something. Do whatever you can, please. I cannot live without him. Bring him here at any cost."

Releasing himself from her grasp, the Guru composed himself and sat down in the posture of meditation. Using his spiritual powers he wanted to know where the boy was and what had detained him. His efforts to locate him did not bear any fruit. It meant that he was not located at one place. Then where was he?, the Guru wondered. He called out loudly,

"Kutch, dear Kutch, my son, come here. We are waiting for you." His repeated calls reverberated through the whole universe. They were not ordinary sounds, but those from an elevated soul who possessed immense powers.

His body parts, lodged inside the wolves soon responded. There was a turbulence within every wolf, which had fed on his body parts. In response to the repeated calls, all the body parts jumped out of their inside and gathered to form a human shape. It was Kutch. He could hear the call of his Guru, resounding in the jungle. He seemed to be waking up from a trance. Raising his hands in the air, he made for the hermitage with the words, "Yes sir, I am coming."

Their joys knew no bounds to see Kutch entering the outer courtyard. The guru was especially excited and relieved because up till now he had experimented his secret powers only on others, and had seen them come to life. It was something mechanical. But in the present case, it was totally different. In him were centred the attachment of both the father and the daughter.

Kutch came running and fell at the feet of the waiting guru. "I'm sorry guruji, for my late return. Kindly pardon me for my mistake."

The guru lifted him up and pressed him to his chest. He was glad to see the boy, returned to his original self. Leaving the guru, he rushed towards the verandah where stood the wonder-struck Devi. She could not help herself clinging to him for satisfaction. It was done in a fit of extreme excitement. To her, the boy had come from the land of the dead.

The news of the revival of the boy had not only caused tremendous embarrassment to the marauders, it had also heightened their anger against the guru.

Now the problem was what to do next. The self-appointed defenders of the land had another meeting to discuss the future move. The news of the boy's killing and his subsequent revival had become the talk of the city. It shocked many as to why a foreign 'vidyarthi' (student) was targeted by the local assailants. What grudge did they have against him? Some of them abhorred at the way, the boy was done to death and his body parts thrown away before wolves to feed on them. It was the height of savagery and perversion. But even greater was the news of the revival of the slain boy by their Guru. They were astonished both at his power of revival and the way the different parts, lodged inside the wolves, had collected to form the original person. It was a curious tale of hatred, savagery, perversion and miracles of the secret 'vidya'. They were certainly aware of the powers of the Guru of reviving the dead soldiers in the battle field, but there the slain persons were mostly intact in their form. But here was a typical case, where a person is killed, hacked into pieces and then his body parts are fed to the hungry wolves. And by the power of the Guru, all the parts jump out of the body of the wolves and collect to form the person he was. It was really a wonder of wonders. Only their Guru was capable of such a miracle.

The merciless killing of an unarmed guiltless boy by a group of unknown assailants deep inside the jungle had given rise to disturbing questions. Granted that the devas were their traditional enemies with whom they had been fighting battles sine times immemorial. But fighting a battle and ambushing a mere boy are two different things. In the former the people are armed and faced with the known enemies, who are almost equal in their might. They also are aware that they have come to fight and settle the scores. But in the latter case, there were many against one: and that too who was innocent, unprepared and unarmed. There was another cause of concern. The boy was an outsider, a sort of guest, the son of the enemy's guru. Being such a one, it was the asuras' sacred duty to see that the boy is done no harm and is duly cared for. They were the enemies of the devas and not the boy's who had not harmed them in any way. Killing such a boy in the horrible manner was an act of national shame. In no way could they justify their dastardly act and defend themselves. It was a slur on their national character. They were thankful to the Guru that he had saved them from their certain ignominy. They could never forget his contribution and they would for ever remain grateful to him.

At the next meeting of the extremists, there was an overview of the current situation along with the general sentiments. The abhorrance caused to the populace at the killing of the boy was discussed and trashed consequently. Such gossip-mongers were dubbed the foolish idealists having no touch with the ground reality. They only talked of ethics, morals, culture, tradition and reputation. They were just a burden on the earth. Defending a country is entirely a different matter. If the country goes to the enemy after a defeat, where will these sweet-tongued idlers go? They had the stupid luxury to talk such big things, because they had nothing to do. People's primary concern ought to be to defend their nation against the enemy. Once the country is secure, only then can people live in peace and prosper in life. A slave country's independence and right to do things as liked, are mortgaged to the alien ruler. Even for its survival it has to struggle.

To the hardliners the sentiments of the moralists were irrelevant and stupid. They just did not matter. As a matter of fact the nation must get preference over every other thing. Even the unethical practices could be condoned for its honour and safety. It was unanimously decided at this meeting that another attempt would be made to do away with the enemy spy. It was just like cancer in their nation's body. It had to be removed at any cost.

Some one came with a radical solution—why not do away both with the Guru and the boy?

"What nonsense do you talk, sir? We are concerned with the boy, not with the Guru. And please explain why the Guru?"

"Yes he is right. Is it not stupid to suggest to kill the Guru? With him shall we also perish."

"How shall we perish, sir?"

"My dear, with his going dead, we shall lose the application of the art and science of Sanjeevani. Then where shall we be in the next battle—with our men killed and none to revive them? I wish the honourable speaker had used his discretion before making such a wild suggestion."

"Yes, yes. It's totally irrelevant and uncalled for."

The first speaker started again, undeterred by the unpalatable comment for his suggestion.

"Dear friends, in your arguments, you lose the sight of the vital question. My feeling is that as long as the Guru lives, the boy will never die however hard we may try and plan."

"How is it, sir?"

"My dear, don't you know that our Guru is an Aryan, a Brahman, the sworn enemy of the asuras. Why should he work for our good? He would rather see to it that we all are decimated."

"Sir, you are talking utter nonsense. We must not be so shameless as to forget the contribution of the Guru, in our last fight against the devas. Does the honourable speaker remember any fight since times immemorial when the asuras had won against the devas? It was only by virtue of the mysterious 'vidya' of the Guru that we could register a victory. As long as the Guru is alive (May he live for hundreds of years!), we shall be victorious. His stay with us is our guarantee of victory."

Thus the last speaker had blasted the theory of killing both of them. It found favour with all. No one could dispute the points.

The most dominant speaker again took the turn. "Gentlemen, let's not waste our time in needless argument, disputing the goodness or weakness of a point. We ought to focus on the most important point—and that's the question of the boy. We have to plan how best to do it so as to settle the matter for ever."

No one could come out with any fresh suggestion, as the best way to deal with the problem had ended in a fiasco. There followed a deafening silence for a while. They had to devise a way to settle things for ever.

"All right, friends. Just now there was a flash in my mind. Last time the body parts were vomited out by the wolves resulting in the regeneration of the dead. They could join together because they were solid in substance. But this time it would not be possible, the way I think."

The people started guessing what better way that could be. They looked at him with curious eyes.

"Friends, this time the Guru will totally fail to restructure the boy. The plan is this. We shall kill the boy and burn him to ashes. After that we shall make a solution of the ashes and mix it with the evening drink of the Guru. As you know, he takes a short drink after the day is done. After he drinks it, the boy would be running through his veins. How could the minutest particles muster up to make a boy?"

All were wondering at the scheme. But it was awfully horrendous and abhorrent. Burning a slain victim, and then mixing his ashes in the sage's drink!! But the people had to gulp it for the sake of their future.

Things were carried out as planned. The killers finished Kutch then burnt his body and collected a handful of ashes in a cup and brought it home.

It was to be mixed with the Guru's drink at the ashram. The Guru had no notion that the drink had been spiked by his own men.

Today also Kutch did not return along with the cows. Why? What had happened? Devyani got jittery. First of all she thought that her fears were baseless, but then she was reminded of the recent talk with her friend who had breathed that some people in the capital were after Kutch's blood and wanted to finish him at any cost. They won't take rest until they had done away with him permanently. They won't mind making any number of attempts to do it. Possibly she was right because this day too he had not returned from the field as yet. She knew how merciless and savage these asuras could be, when it comes to killing. But it did not appeal to her. Some one in her heart said that the asuras had already killed him in the past. And they had seen that there was no effect of decimating him, as he had been revived by the Guru. So it was useless to do it. Considering the futility of the cruel exercise, they might give up their plan.

But it wasn't like that. Even our best and solid arguments are shattered at the rock of reality. Fear of his death again overtook her. It had rubbished all her previous positive thoughts. Evan an unpleasant truth sometimes proves to be real.

"Father, Kutch hasn't returned till now. What's happened to him? He is not a time-waster and an irresponsible person. He would have come back without any delay. Father dear, I genuinely fear for his life. These asuras have killed him again as he is their greatest eye sore.

"Worry not dear, your fears are baseless. The asuras won't be so stupid as to kill him again, knowing that it was a useless exercise. It would never help them."

"Father dear, I want to believe your words but my sixth sense says that the savages have killed him again otherwise tell me, why has he not come back yet?"

What could the sage answer? Although he had tried to calm her down by discounting her fears, in the heart of his own hearts, he had a feeling that the unpredictable asuras had played another dirty game with the poor boy. Himself he tried to look calm and normal, but Devyani could see that his efforts to look so were ineffective. He was equally worried. His eyes told that. -----------------

As the night advanced, the Guru advised Devyani to retire to bed and not to worry unnecessarily. The boy would be back the next day, he was sure. But she did not want to go. Where had Kutch gone after all? Where could he spend the night? He was a stranger after all in that area? But when she noticed her father retiring into his room, she too had to. Intense pain and suffering in the present brought to her mind the past dew unforgettable moments of her life. In painful days the pleasant thoughts of the past tend to soften the intensity and create a sense of false comfort.

She could not help remembering the night when it was raining hard and thundering. Since her childhood, she had been dead scared of lightning and thunder, and would rush to the comfort of her father's bed. To day scared by the frequent lightning and thunder, she crept into Kutch's room, thinking that he would be studying his lessons in the study room. She thought of staying there, until the natural furies had subsided. His bed was not as cosy but she had no other option. She did not know when sleep overtook her. Darkness is very congenial to sleep: light disturbs.

Kutch was stunned to find Devyani in his bed. How could she come here! It had never been so. He tried to wake her up, but she won't.

Fatigued with various kinds of mental and physical activities, he sat at the far end of the bed for sometime and spread himself lengthwise thereafter. He was awakened by a soft touch on his back and shoulder, but shrugged it off.

Devyani was mumbling something. Was she dreaming? He ignored it and relapsed into his dream world. Lying next to him, felt so warm and reassuring to her. His physical proximity seemed to be stoking her fantasies. After a while she realized what a blunder she had committed. It was immoral to be there. She woke up, and in the misty light of the dawn tried to look at his face. By this time the sky had cleared of the dark clouds and visibility had improved. Soon she scurried to her room. The feelings of the last few moments in that room had been etched on her mind.

Today, she woke up with a start. The cruel memories of the last night were haunting her. When would he return? When could she see his face? Perhaps there was no hope of his return. He had been lost for ever. Last time her father had revived him and he had returned from the world of the dead. But was it not a fluke? The 'vidya' was not working this time. The thought of never seeing him made her distraught. What have gods willed for me, she said.

The next morning failed to bring back the boy. There was despondency and desperation in the air. The Guru was feeling unusually upset. So many hours are gone, and no trace of the boy! Shouldn't he try to apply the secret art? If not now, then when? He called Kutch's name repeatedly. But no materialization yet! He was getting desperate. A few more calls were given. But the response was different this time. There was a turmoil and turbulence inside his own body. The boy was alive in every drop of his blood and was travelling through his nerves. The calls acted upon the drops. They started gelling together in various lumps. After continuous throbbing in his body, a human form emerged out of the Guru's body. Kutch was standing before him----reborn. Wasn't it another miracle! Both Shukracharya and Devyani saw it, in addition to some more souls who had come there to sympathise at the boy's disappearance.

Seeing the figure bending before him for paying his regards, the Guru said, "My dear, this is your second birth. And since you are born out of me, you are my second child. You are welcome."

Kutch had no knowledge what all had happened during the intervening period. But he was excited to hear that his Guru had called him his own child. Up till now he had been treated only as an adopted one. It was different now as he was born out of him. The sage too was relieved that the boy was not lost, and he won't have to cut a sorry figure before his friend Brihaspati. No more would there be a sense of guilt, haunting him every moment. He asked Kutch to relax and not to stir out that day. In his opinion he needed some rest.

The conspirators felt themselves completely defeated. Neither of their schemes had worked. Even in the distant future, they did not visualize any scheme which could succeed. Their Guru will always come in the way of their success. So they resigned themselves to their fate.

Sometimes it happens that we don't get results despite the best of our methods and efforts. And that is called Destiny. There is no use fighting against it. Things will happen as they are destined to be, howsoever hard we try. So the only option left was to let the boy stay as long as he wanted, and then return to his father's 'lok'.

Their efforts to save their race from total destruction had miserably failed. It seemed as if gods themselves were not in favour of their well-being and their survival. The sad fact was that the boy would be able to steal the secret knowledge from their Guru, and they all would be letting it happen as helpless spectators. Everything seemed to be working against them. They ultimately realized that there was no decree against fate. What is fated, cannot be blotted.

14

The Departure

DUE TO THE CESSATION OF the wicked schemes and any other form of interference, the process of Kutch's learning and assimilation went on smoothly in the coming years. Now Kutch had a feeling that there was nothing more to learn from the Guru: no more queries to make. All his doubts had been clarified by the learned one in course of the lessons.

However, as a matter of courtesy he politely enquired of him whether he planned to cover any more field, the Guru replied that there was nothing left.

Then Kutch asked, "Now that my lessons are complete, may I go back home, sir?"

"Yes, dear, there is no harm. You can go home as and when you wish. Your people must be anxiously waiting for you.", said the Guru.

But all this happened without the knowledge of Devyani. When she noticed that Kutch was packing up his belongings, she wondered what he was doing.

"What are you doing, dear?"

"Packing up for my return."

"Why?"

"Because I've finished my education. Guruji has said that there is nothing more to teach. He had taught me all that he knew."

"But how can you go?"

"Why? Why can't I go? I had come here with a mission. And that is complete. Where is the need to prolong my stay?"

Devyani was lightning-struck. She had never thought that the youth with whom she had spent the recent years of adulthood, whom she had adored, and around whom she had woven dreams of staying for life, would leave her behind and go away.

She begged of him to change his decision. "Dear Kutch, please don't go. Stay here with us. I am quite lonely. Your company kept me happy. I'd always thought you had come here for ever."

Kutch kept on looking at her distraught face and stood motionless. He had finished his packing.

"Kutch dear, you are my love, my god. I had always dreamt of staying with you. Without you, there is no life. I'll kill myself."

"Come on Devi, don't be silly. Don't be unnecessarily emotional and sentimental. Let's face facts."

"What facts!How can you be so cruel, so ruthless and so heartless?"

"Dear, your problem arises because you don't want to face the facts. You are being carried away by your dreams and your fantasies."

"Yes, I am not as cruel and indifferent as you. I have a heart. I am not a statue without emotions."

"My dear, emotions and heart are great things. But hey have their own place in our lives. They can't stand before the facts and duty."

"What facts and duty, Kutch? Don't you owe anything to us? We looked after all your needs and comforts. We never allowed you to feel lonely and uncomfortable. Father treated you as his own child. Shouldn't you have regards for our feelings?"

"Dear Devi, there's no denying the fact that both of you looked after me so well. I never felt I was a stranger. But please remember that I had come here for learning at the feet of the Guru. And now when that is done, I must go back. People at home must be waiting for me."

Devyani found Kutch adamant. None of her emotional pleadings had any impact on him. She was not at all prepared for this situation. The very thought of separating from him was death to her. It would be the end of her world.

Overcome with grief and helplessness in persuading him, she became desperate. She could not help herself throwing her arms around the man standing before her and say, "My dear, Kutch, I cannot live without you. I love you. I have always looked upon you as the man in my life, as my spouse, as my husband."

"You've been insisting on going back because of the fact that you were a stranger. You had no blood relation. But if I became your consort, you will be related to us. And then family ties would press you to stay."

Her hold round him was getting tighter. She was in no mood to loosen it, nor was she in a mood to let him go. Kutch was in a quandary. What to do? It was getting both embarrassing and ugly. He was torn between the alternatives—to return to 'devlok' or to stay here? If he went away, the girl would kill herself out of love for him and he would be held guilty of driving her to suicide because of his rigidity. He wanted to deter her. But how?

Trying to release himself from her grip, he said softly, "Dear Devyani, you think you love me and I do not. That is wrong. Nothing could be farther from the truth. I too dreamt of having a wife like you who would have made my life blissful. But the circumstances are not favourable."

"How's that, Kutch!", she came closer again to him. She showed some positive signs. Her curiosity multiplied and she looked at him.

"Dear Devi, marriage is possible between the persons of two different families."

"Yes, so are we. You came from 'devlok' and I belong to asurlok. Moreover, our families and parents are different."

"Yes, Devi. It's like that. But today the circumstances are different from what they were yesterday. You must not forget the difference between the past and the present."

Devyani was non-plussed. What was the young man saying? How could the past be different from the present? Whatever was there in the past, continues to be in the present.

"What do you mean, Kutch? You have puzzled me. I just don't understand you. How could the present and past be different?"

Placing his hands on her shivering shoulders, he said, "Dear Devyani, we cannot marry because we are siblings—brother and sister."

She looked at him with utter disbelief. What was the man saying?

Kutch continued, "Devyani, when I came here from 'swarglok', I was born of my parents there, but now the situation is changed.

She looked at him with unbelieving eyes.

"Remember, when I was revived for the second time, I was born out of your father's body. After my materialization, he had said that because I had been produced out of him, I was his child. Thus both of us are his children."

Devyani was lightning-struck. She could not believe her ears. She just did not want to although she remembered that her father had said so at his second revival. Sometimes truth is extremely cruel and disastrous. It has no regards for an individual's feelings and well-being.

Whatever Kutch had said was too unpalatable to digest. She felt floored. Her world was broken to pieces before her own eyes. How wicked this man is!! How cruel! an ungrateful wretch!! Now that his mission is complete, he feels that he has succeeded and he has befooled us. Actually he has taken undue advantage of our goodness and hospitality.

Kutch had fired the last and most potent weapon in his arsenal i.e. of their incompatibility due to blood relations.

"What a blackguard! what a cheat!" Devyani could see her boat sinking in the turbulent sea. Even after many attempts she was unable to save it. The matter was slipping out of her hand! Oh what a luck!!

Although their incompatibility was established on the basis of the bare facts, Devyani was still unable to accept it and come to terms. What an irony! that knowing the truth, one is not ready to acknowledge it.

All this drama was being enacted in the ashram while the Guru was away. He had been summoned by the king for an important discussion and guidance. Moreover, he had permitted the boy to return in his absence. He did not want to withhold him without any reason. A disciple returns home at the conclusion of his course. There was nothing unusual in it.

Finding that Kutch was bent upon proceeding despite her prayers and allurements, Devyani outstretched her both hands sideways, stopping him from going out of the cottage door.

"Kutch, dear, you can't go, leaving me behind. I cannot live without you. Please break your promise and stay with me for my sake. It's sinful to reject a maiden's offer. God's curse falls upon such a person. Even our Shastras say so."

Kutch was not to be deterred and beaten by her argument. He was adamant as before. Pushing her aside, he wanted to make his way. At this Devyani could not contain herself and exploded,

"All right, Kutch go as you wish to. You have insulted and cheated us, and abused our hospitality. You are a blackguard. You had come here with the intentions of learning the secret 'vidya' of Sanjeevni from my father. Now that your wish is fulfilled, you are going away shamelessly. You have deeply hurt us: you'll have to pay for it.

"I hereby curse you that the secret 'vidya' you have leaarnt from your Guru, will be of no avail to you in time of emergency. It will be just off your mind." Her eyes were red with anger and seemed to be sending out flames.

Kutch remained stupefied and unmoved. But he wasn't to be cowed down or demoralized. Of course, he was mortified to hear the curse. If his new-found knowledge would be of no use in times of need, then what was the outcome of his trip to the asurlok!! Every effort he had made up till now was going to be nullified by her few angry words.

Kutch thought of its consequences back home. How crestfallen everyone would be!! Their hopes would be shattered. They were doubly sure that their boy hero was coming back with a prized possession. But no, this was not going to happen.

The thought of the futility of his 'tapasya' filled him with uncontrollable rage. By temperament he was a cool-headed person, never given to tantrums, but it was unusual. The dreams of his people, their expectations, and the futility of his sincere endeavour got the better of him and he shot back,"

"Devi, it does not behove you to curse me thus, nullifying all my efforts and the 'swadhyaya'. However, if you think it right, let it be so. After all I am glad that I had to learn many more things from the Guru, than only that 'vidya'.

"Remember, your curse comes out of your frustration for not having me as your partner, your spouse. There is no other pious reason. You are blinded by your idle passions, your carnal desires and your romantic ideas of life. It was your own fault to be infatuated with me. I never reciprocated your amorous overtures. I always ignored them as I had come here with a pious mission for my people. You kept on with your idle pursuits, because you had nothing better to do than indulge in the game of romance. You were always guided by your baser instincts, never ever gauging what the other man was thinking about you. Your efforts were a one-way traffic. You fancied and made castles in the air, without ever realizing the truth. It was your fault. You are therefore, responsible for your grief and unhappiness and none else. Come on, and make way and let me go."

But the distraught Devyani would not budge. She turned hysterical.

"Devyani, as you have cursed me undeservedly and have hurt me grievously, I too am hereby compelled to curse you. No Brahman boy will ever ask for your hands, and you will remain unmarried for long. Ultimately, you will be married outside your fold—to a lower caste. And that would be a matter of grave family disgrace."

Saying so, Kutch grew physical and pushing her aside, scurried out into the open courtyard for his onward journey.

Pushed by Kutch, Devyani gave out a loud shriek and slumped on the floor with a thud.

SECTION--- II

1

A New Beginning

AFTER THE EMOTIONAL STORM HAD blown over, there followed a period of relative peace and serenity. Devyani realized the futility of living in the past as it doesn't help. One should look at it only for the sake of learning a lesson for the coming days. Grieving over the loss is sheer stupidity.

Her bitterness towards Kutch was gradually ebbing away. While having an overview of the things in the past, which had tormented her so much, she found that to a great extent she was herself to blame. Her infatuation for Kutch had blinded her so much that she had refused to see things in the right perspective. Hers was a one-sided affair. When had she found him reciprocating her pleasing overtures? He merely ignored them or smiled indifferently. It was her fault that she had mistaken his diffidence and shyness for his approval. But silence or unresponsiveness does not mean that the other person approves of it. She had often pinched his cheeks, pushed him physically, put her hands on his shoulders, garlanded him too, but he seemed to be unaffected by all this.

He did not even take undue advantage of the moments when she had slipped into his bed on a stormy night of lightning and thunder. She was, as she had told him later, dead scared of such horrible nights and at such moments she sought someone's protection. But as for herself, she was thrilled by the very thought of his proximity in the bed.

She pitied herself at the loss of her ability to think for degrading herself and her dear father. She should not have begged of the unwilling Kutch to marry her and settle for ever in the 'asurlok'. Wasn't it inappropriate and ugly for the daughter of a respectable Guru to conduct like that? Where was her self respect, her modesty and her father's respect? Had all her prayers and begging at his feet not resulted in nothing? O, how low a person can fall when blinded by lust!! She was sad that she had been overtaken by her violent passion and had done things which were unwarranted.

But life doesn't end only after one stormy affair. It has to move on further and go on. She vowed to herself to conduct herself more responsibly and discreetly in future and prove worthy of her father. It was lucky that all this emotional drama was enacted in the absence of the old man. He had been invited by the king for an important session. How mortified would he have been, if he had witnessed his daughter conducting herself so indecently?

Devyani seemed to have passed through an 'agnipariksha' (a fire- ordeal) and felt that she had been reborn. The whole of the stormy and ugly past was now a chapter of history. She would not allow it to taint her present.

She started her life afresh with the usual enthusiasm, breeziness, and cheerfulness. She was socializing with her ashram friends again. They did not suspect any wrong to have happened to her. If she was meeting them less than often in the preceding years, it was mainly due to her diverse domestic chores, and time spent in conversations with Kutch. Any one could see that. But at times she was given to bouts of melancholy and depression.

Guru Shukracharya's experienced eyes could not miss the changes in his daughter. He had brought her up as an indulgent parent and was therefore, conversant with her temperament and slight mood shifts. Feeling of sadness at the departure of the boy, with whom she had spent several adolescent years, was not unnatural. As a matter of fact he himself was subjected to sadness at his departure. During the last few years, the lad had become a part and parcel of his family. He had endeared himself to all and sundry. The Guru comforted her and tried to remove her despondency. He had noted that her old friends in the ashram could not cheer her up and revive her chirpiness. As her father, he could not see her unhappy. She was the only purpose in his life. He must do something for her, he thought.

The anxieties for his daughter could not help tainting his demeanour. He looked unusually taut, tense and morose.

King Vrisparva had noticed it. Initially he took it for something, owing to personal reasons and a passing phase, but it had prolonged curiously. If he was not comfortable himself, how could his counsel be sound. It would affect the administration too. He therefore, decided to make a dent.

"Respected Sir, you don't look cheerful and normal these days. Is there any reason to worry? I wish I had been of some help in making things easier for you," said the worried king.

"No your excellency, there is nothing serious."

"Still your honour, you look disturbed."

"Dear King, it's of personal nature. It's too trifling to deserve your attention."

"Gurudeva, for you it might be trifling, but it is certainly troubling your soul. Kindly be good enough to share your problem with me, if that be not so confidential."

"O dear king, my anxiety is on account of my daughter. She has attained the marriageable age. Being a father, it's my sincere wish to find a suitable match for her. My anxieties are typical of a father having nubile kids. I shall be relieved, once she is settled."

The king readily agreed. He said, "Gurudeva, the world is full of suitable young men, and there is no dearth of such ones. We shall henceforth be on the look out for a suitable guy. No one knows when we would get one. Destiny plays a vital role in such matters, Guruji. I pray to you to be patient and wait for the right moment."

"Yes, king Vrish, you've said it well. But my anxiety is also related to her day to day engagements. She feels terribly lonely at home with none to talk to and share her feelings. There is not much of domestic work too these days which could keep her occupied. The girls on the ashram complex no longer interest her: some are too young and some too boring. She yearns for an intelligent company.

"The other reason is my constant concern for her safety. Being grown up and charming is something good. But it's not safe for such a girl to live alone for long hours. You know the society. There are so many evil eyes. How long can I keep a watch on her? For obvious reasons, I cannot stay at home all the time."

"Honourable Gurudeva, your concerns and anxieties are quite natural. Any one in your position would think like that. Actually she suffers from loneliness more acutely, because there is no lady at home. Had her mother been alive, she would have taken care of her. A grown up girl can't share her innermost feelings with a male member of the family whether brother or father. There are some tender and sensitive matters which she cannot share with them.

"I had offered your honour a residence in the palace complex, but you refused the offer and preferred to stay in the far away ashram complex. May I request you again to shift to that building immediately? Staying on the palace complex will take care of your concern for her safety, and it would be close to us too."

"Thanks for the offer, king Vrish. I am inclined to yield to your offer. But I shall not go for a magnificent structure. I shall prefer a small house, preferably a cottage. I shall feel more at home in a simple dwelling. A big house is intimidating and too artificial."

"All right, Guruji. A little away from the royal premises, there is a cluster of woods with some ashrams for the priests. A suitable ashram will be raised there in a day or two for you to shift.

"My daughter, Sharmistha, too will get a suitable company in your daughter. She too is almost of the same age. I am sure they will soon be able to gell with each other and find the company pleasant."

Shukracharya was pleased on both the counts: the ashram near the royal palace would help him in attending to his duties and would also guarantee the safety of Devyani. On the other hand, king Vrishparva's daughter too would be friends with his daughter. What better arrangement could be there than this? It was meeting all the requirements.

2

In the New Surrounding

THE CHANGE OF PLACE HAD its own advantages. While life became more convenient for the Guru, Devyani too got new faces to look at. The memories associated with the recent tragic happenings did not torment her here. Our memories are time and place related. When we move out of the surroundings, we tend to forget them. A new place has its own charm. Mind also starts thinking and planning how best to adjust there. This sort of acclimatization tends to wear away the old layers of sorrows and sufferings.

The girl had a fresh lease of life so to say, in the new surroundings. The place was more likeable because she had princess Sharmishtha, the daughter of king Vrishparva, for her friend. The king himself had taken initiative in introducing her to Devyani. They became friendly not only because they were of the same age, their likes and dislikes too matched. They spent most of their waking hours in the company of each other. Sometimes Devyani would come to the royal apartments of the princess, and stay for hours and sometimes the princess would go to the ashram hermitage to spend time with her. The surroundings of the one was very dear to the other. So when the princess came to the ashram precincts, she enjoyed the open air environment, the sight of clump of trees, the deer and their fawns, the peacock and other birds in their natural state, the sight of a river with its banks where the ashram dwellers would go with their families for a bath and wash. The sight of the young children swimming in the river, frolicking there and throwing water at each other while bathing was very enjoyable. She particularly liked the swing in the courtyard. Sometimes one would push the swing a few times, while the other was seated, and sometimes both would be seated. It was thrilling to go high into the air. The pleasures of being in the air for a while was beyond description. One felt as if he had cut off his relations with mother earth. It was so exciting.!!

In the season of spring, when the whole ashram was in blooms all around with all kinds of flowering plants in their youthful splendour, life became exceedingly colourful. Such a thing was not to be found in the palace. Life within the high walls seemed to be adtificial. The princess did not have the freedom to move wherever she liked. Everywhere there were restrictions, royal guards and all that. One could not do what one desired. There were so many do's and don'ts. But in the ashram it was so different!!

Visits to the ashrams were more enjoyable because there was a friend like Devyani there. It seemed as if both had been made for each other. The similarities between them were tremendous. They liked to wear the same kind of clothes, the same colours, the same shades, the same designs: their choice of food too was similar. They liked to sing songs together while swinging in the air or preparing garlands and other ornaments of flowers for self-embellishment. Sometimes the princess would come to the ashram quite early in the morning and stay for long hours. They wanted to make the most of their time together. The idea of separating from the other was so painful. But they would promise to each other to be together again. The princess found playing various local games in the ashram courtyard quite absorbing and enjoyable. Here the royal guards were not there to restrict her freedom and activities. She often told her father that she did not require any security in the ashram, as there was no threat of any kind to her life. She also told him that she could not enjoy her company with Devyani, as she always felt that she was under the gaze of the royal guards. And that robbed them of their pleasures.

The king too saw reason in it. His daughter really needed freedom to enjoy herself. In the ashram, there was no such threat. He too was an indulgent father like the Guru. Their daughters were the apples of their eyes. They did not want to stand in the way to their pleasures.

Both of the friends had decided that they would spend the "Vasantotsava" (the spring festival) together in the ashram compound. There could not be any better place for celebrating the Spring festival. Because here the nature was in full bloom: there were no restrictions on their movement. Both had decided that in the morning they would go out to pluck flowers, then they would prepare garlands, armlets, bracelets, ear rings with the flowers for themselves. And after visiting the local temple, they would play with colour and smear each other's face along with those of the ashramites. To make the day memorable and to look the prettiest on the day, they would put on a particular dress of a particular hue. Devyani's father always bought the kinds of dress for her as the princess wore. Why should they look different or inferior to the other? Any sort of mismatch would be a thorn in the flesh.

3

The Ugly Tiff

THE DAY OF 'VASANTOTSAVA,' FOR which they had waited and planned things so impatiently had ultimately dawned. The princess woke up earlier than usual and after making herself fresh post ablutions, left for the hermitage with a handmaid. She was carrying the princess' personal effects. Devyani was surprised at her arrival. It was so early! Things could wait. But it would provide them opportunity to stay together for longer hours. Sharmistha asked her handmaid to return to the palace and report to the queen about her day's programme. The handmaid could come again to escort her back before the sun down.

Soon Deavani performed the domestic chores and informed her father about the day's engagements with the princess. She did not want to make her friend wait for nothing. What would she think about her? That Devyani was not as much impatient as she was. That would be improper. She too took out her new dress for the day, and showed to her father. He was glad that his daughter was going to have a nice time. He smiled at her approvingly.

With songs on their lips and music in their hearts, the girls left for the first job of the day: collection of the choicest flowers for their flowery ornaments. There were so many varieties of the blooms: rose, marigold, night queen, jasmine etc among the sweet-smelling and several among without fragrance. Their bags were soon overflowing with the blooms. On their return home, they got occupied with preparing ornaments for themselves. Their nimble fingers were doing wonders with the blooms. The ornaments were taking the desired shapes. Along with these shapes were they also imagining how pretty they would be looking with these ornaments! Their natural charms would be greatly enhanced. Guru Shukracharya did not stay with them as he had his own customary engagements. The king must be having his own programme for this festive occasion. Moreover, his presence at home would be a sort of impediment for the girls. They would not be doing things as freely as they would like.

They soon felt it was getting late for the 'colour throwing' function. They readied themselves for that. By that time other ashram girls too had gathered there for the most awaited ritual. They were joined by the duo, who were themselves so impatient about it. One could see them running here and there to avoid the smearing of colours, but they could not evade their friends in hot chase. When the evaders were overpowered, they were treated the way they deserved. Liberal smearing of the dry colours on their wet bodies and the face had made them unrecognizable. The session of the dry colours was followed by thorough 'bath' with wet colours. In the end they all looked gruesome and monstrous. As the colours were prepared only with flowers and various fragrant herbs, they did not afflict their eyes or caused any sort of skin irritation.

Even too much of merriment and pleasure makes us jaded. A moment comes when the person finds that the things that had given pleasures up till now, no longer interest him. He is bored and wishes to engage himself otherwise. This had happened with these boisterous girls. Now was the time to stop all this merry-making and go home. Before going home it was unanimously decided that for bathing and washing themselves, they would go to the river bank and clean themselves together. Removing the layers of heavy colours on the skin was a herculean task. It would take much longer than the usual bath. The river bath was the most appropriate thing to do. Soon they dispersed and proceeded from their homes to the river with their clothes. Every body would like to put on their best on the festive occasion. Their flashy garments were meant for this.

Community bath at the river was another occasion for merry-making. It was actually the extension of their colour-throwing, smearing spree. They had plenty of frolicking in the water. It was a game to splash water on each other and swim for short stretches. Those who were scared of this adventure, were helped by those who were skilled in the art. They would be encouraged to beat their hands and feet in the water to keep themselves afloat, and swim for a short stretch. In this exercise not all were as adventurous and courageous. But on the whole they enjoyed themselves. It was a rare occasion for all girls to get together. They wanted to make the most of it. Let it be etched in their memory.

It was breezy when they had started. The wind is usually soft in the spring season. But sometimes the weather turns foul without any reason. It was like that today. Dark clouds had started gathering while the girls were enjoying themselves in the river, but by god's grace it did not last long. It was blown away by a strong wind. Soon the weather was clear. When the girls came one after another they found that their garments had got mixed up with each other. It took time in disengaging one set from the other. Devyani came earlier than her friend. The other was still enjoying her time in the river. She had just learnt a few swimming strokes. Beating the water surface with her limbs gave her indescribable pleasure. Her friend was calling her from the bank but she would not listen. When would she get an opportunity to swim and bathe in the river water again? The palace people would have never permitted that. Here there was no one to restrain her. By that time Devyani had cast off her wet clothes and changed into the new ones. For a moment she was confused which pieces belonged to her, because her friend's set looked very much like hers even though there was a subtle difference.

Whiling coming out of the river, Sharmistha stumbled on the bank, and sprained her leg. It was not a major injury though, but it was painful. She too wanted to be dressed into her new resplendent clothes soonest possible. Devyani had done it already. Devyani was sorry to see that while all were well, her friend had sustained an injury. But such things happen. No one can stop it. An accident is an accident and can happen to any one at any time. Because of her injury, she needed assistance. Devyani helped her change her clothes. The wet clothes had to be cast off first and wrung for draining the water.

While putting on her clothes, Sharmistha had a feeling that there was something wrong with her set. It was not hers that she was wearing: her clothes had a different feel: different texture and different smoothness. Being habituated of wearing costly clothes, she had an uncanny understanding of the texture. Born and brought amidst luxury and abundance any one in her position could easily know which object is classy and which is not. Her gut feeling prevailed on her. Her pain which had partially incapacitated her movements had made her irritable. And the suspicion that her friend had cheated her by wearing her set made her immensely enraged. How could Devyani do it? Didn't she know that it was her set? Didn't she know the quality of her cloth? Didn't she feel the difference when she had put it on? She must have done it willfully. But she kept her feeling of displeasure to herself. The thoughts of having been cheated made her inspect Devyani's clothes more closely. She was standing all this while, helping her in her dress change. The more she looked, the more she got infuriated. To her, all the love and affection shown by Devyani was just a sham. She was actually a cheat and a blackguard at heart. She only posed what she was not.

Devyani had noticed that her friend was not as cheerful as she temperamentally was. What had made such a chirpy and happy girl so diffident and morose? Was the pain so unbearable that she was trying to get over it? But it is simply a minor sprain. It's not serious. Then what could be the reason? By this time she had finished the change. It's better to ask her what ails her.

They had spent a lot of time on the river bank. Now it was time to return home. On the way Devyani thought of broaching the matter.

"Dear Shary (she called her by this name as she called her 'Devi') you are not looking happy. Anything wrong? Does the injury pain you much?"

"No Devi, I 'm okay."

"No dear, you can't hide your feelings from me. We have lived together for so long, how can we not gauge what worries the other? Come on, tell me. The physical pain is different from the mental pain, I know. The face shows it."

Sharmistha was not in a mood to give out the reason for her displeasure. She was too full of the thoughts of being befooled and cheated by her own friend. If she was persisting, it was better to let her know how she had dealt unfairly with her. Such sort of treatment was just not expected. It was awful.

"Come on Devi, please share your cause of displeasure. It's getting on my nerves."

Sharmistha could not contain herself. She felt like exploding and she did in an uncharacteristic fashion. "Devi, only today did I realize that your love and affection for me is but a sham."

Devyani was stunned. She kept on looking at her dear friend as to what she meant. "My dear, what are you saying! Do you understand what it all means? I, believing in double dealing! Gods, what is my friend saying! O.k. how did you come to this conclusion, dear?" Devyani looked hurt. In fact her love for her friend was transparent like the water in a pool.

"Devi, being the daughter of a sage you were always envious of me, my lot, my status and my personal effects. In the heart of your hearts you never wanted me to be so happy. But you could not help. I was born like that in a royal family and had everything I could wish."

"I wonder Shary, why such weird thoughts have come to your mind all of a sudden. Never even for a moment did I think that you will have such a low opinion about your bosom friend. I beg of you to please tell me what has caused this change in you."

"Devyani, remember, opinion about a person is not formed just in a day. It is accumulated on the basis of the instances in the past. Through your eyes I could make out what your secret feelings were. I remember how strangely you behaved when you came to our royal apartments."

"Honestly I have never thought like that. The world is full of people of all sorts; some are rich by birth, whereas some are poor. It's not their fault. What makes the difference is their way of thinking. Even a rich person could think like a beggar, and a beggar can think like the rich."

The comparison of beggar and rich seemed to be a direct reference to her, as Sharmistha felt. It was too bitter a comparison to digest. She felt terribly offended. Then she must say what was troubling her mind. Things were getting ugly.

"Don't forget Devi, that you envied me for my dress for today's festival. The pieces are so magnificent. In comparison to them, yours were poor and inferior stuff. I had noticed the jealousy in your eyes when I had come to your ashram with my maid. I cannot forget a certain glaze in your eyes when you saw my set. You looked so depressed and defeated. And since then you had the intention to grab it at any cost."

"Shary, it is your illusion. Poor I might be, but I never felt greedy of any unfair gain. My 'sanskaras' (grooming) are not like that. In fact all the motives that you have imputed on me till now are reflective of an arrogant mind. You always had a feeling of being a king's daughter. You always thought that by making friends with me, you were obliging me, elevating me, trying to show to the world how that you have no airs about being a princess."

It seemed to be a direct attack on her. Sharmistha could not gulp it.

"You are trying to show how cultured you are, then why did you put on my set of clothes, Devi? Didn't you have a sense that the set was not yours? Are you so naive that you are unable to distinguish between two entirely different sets? I know how deep you are! You had thought that you will put on my dress on the pretext that they had got mixed up due to the strong wind, and in a hurry you could not find the difference. You also knew that once you have put it on, I would not accept it, and naturally it would be yours."

The blame game was getting dirtier. Sharmistha was unnecessarily blaming her for the things that never were. She had been doubting her very motive. She was still not sure that she was actually wearing her friend's dress. They were so similar! And even if she had done so, as her good friend she should have pointed it out in good faith. Why should she have talked about her motive, her lower social status? No she had a wrong opinion about her friend.

"Come on, Devi. You could not pretend that you could not distinguish between the clothes. One can say the difference by the very feel of it, when one touched it or held in the hand. But you did it under the pretext of feigned ignorance."

They were still moving home ward and had covered some distance: but it was still far from the palace complex. Their quarrels had impeded their pace.

Sharmistha was repeatedly humiliating her 'once dear' friend. But there is a limit to which you can take abuses and insult. Anger was building up inside Devyani. It was getting worse every moment. Being displeased, she gave a push to Sharmistha. It was only to show her anger, but the push made her stumble, and she fell in a lump. Had she been all right, the push won't have unbalanced her. She would have remained steady. But the injury in the leg had a debilitating effect. She could not control herself and gave out a painful cry. It pained her mentally too. Devyani knew it well that she was injured in the leg, and every step she was taking needed effort. Even then she had given her a push. It was certainly done with an ulterior motive i.e. to give her trouble. A real friend would never have done so. She would have realized her predicament. What sort of sympathy could she expect from her? She was behaving like a sworn enemy.

Seeing her slump at her push, Devyani felt guilty. She never wanted to harm her. She knew that she was already in pain. But her arrow-like sharp words had injured her heart. She had made every effort to insult and humiliate her. She tried to lend a hand of support to Sharmistha to get up but she jerked it. Faking sympathy after the push!! Still she was supported. She needed a little rest. Nearby they noticed the parapet of the blind well. It had dried up years ago. People said that its underground stream, which supplied water had dried up so there was no water in it. They could sit on the parapet of the well for a while. The rest could provide some relief........

Sharmistha still seemed to be in a bad temper. "Devi, didn't you prove that your love for me was a mere show? You knew of my injury, even then you pushed me. Why? Won't it add to my pain? A true friend would never have done so. She would feel the pain of her friend and make every effort to comfort her. Actually only I am to blame myself for my misfortunes and my bad judgment. I made friends with a person like you which you never deserved. Even otherwise, where is the ground of friendship between us? We are socially so apart. You (are) the child of a Brahman, who subsists at the mercy of my father, who is of no avail if my father withdraws his patronage. Why should I have made friends with his child? It has been rightly said that friendship always prospers between the equals. It was a blunder on my part to have treated you as my equal.

The quarrel had become too personal. Sharmistha was continually insulting and demeaning her. She was full of venom. Why should she use such uncharitable expressions for my father? He does not subsist on the king's patronage. The king had himself invited him to be his mentor and advisor. It was only by virtue of her father that the asuras had vanquished the devas, the traditional victors. She is so ungrateful and mean. Her offensive darts had injured her immensely. The princess had left no stone unturned to humiliate her. This should have been avoided. There is a limit of decency which we mustn't cross howsoever angry we might be. But the princess was in a mood to fight to finsh.

Overcome with rage, Devyani stood up from the parapet and grabbed Sharmistha by the shoulders. She wanted to give her a violent shake to express her grave displeasure. The other took this gesture of hers as a physical onslaught on her and therefore, slapped her for her audacity to touch a princess!! It was a state of unsavoury agitation, wherein the duo had grabbed each other and was intent on having the better of the other. It had resulted in a show of strength. They forgot they were sitting on the parapet of a well. One of them could fall into it. And that happened. A violent jolt from Sharmistha unsteadied Devyani. And while she was trying to regain her balance, the princess pushed her, knowing not that it was a dangerous act. But we lose our ability to judge things in a state of uncontrollable rage.

The casualty of her rage was Devyani. She gave out a shriek while tumbling into the blind well. Thank God it was dry, otherwise she would have been drowned. Her fall woke up Sharmistha to the gravity of situation. What had she done to her bosom friend! What will the people say? What will her parents say about their lovable daughter? Would they believe that she had done such a ghastly thing? After hearing her they will chastise her and blame her for her rashness which could be fatal. How could she face the world? If the people came to know, what would they think of her? That such a simple girl, and such a ghastly deed!! Her rashness of temper would be the subject of people's talk! It was therefore, appropriate to hide somewhere in the palace where she could not be found. There were so many chambers there. Who knows where she was hiding. But how long could she hide? That did not occur to her. Her present concern was to avoid the people's gaze. And if they did not see her, how could they question?

4

Rescue from the Hell Hole

THERE WAS ANXIETY IN THE palace that Sharmistha had not returned from the ashram yet. By this time the festivities should have been over. A messenger was set off to check why she had not returned. What was the delay? But she was not to be found. In fact she had already come back to the royal apartments and hidden herself. She had made it sure that no body noticed her. She was aware of the nooks and corners where one could not be noticed. And she had succeeded in her venture. There was a certain unease every where. It was the question of the princess's safety. The guards and the spies were on their toes................

If the people in the palace complex were worried about the trace of the princess, here in the ashram the Guru too was worried. Where had the apple of his eye disappeared? Supposing she had gone to the palace with her friend, she should have been back by now. She knew how her father would call her by name, as soon as he returned home. She was aware of his personal needs. She would tend to them immediately. The unusual absence was the cause of his anxiety. How long could he wait? Should he go to the palace himself and check the things? But it was indecent. It would speak of his weakness. After all he was the king's advisor: he had his status. He must conduct himself in accordance with the desired norms. He must wait until she is back. Soon the sun would set....The sage kept on brooding.

<hr />

It was lucky that the fall into the well did not harm Devyani as much as it would have done, had there been no thick layers of vegetation in the pit. She had landed on them with a mighty thud, but due to the cushion that they provided, she remained unhurt. But the problem was who would notice that she was lying here in the pit of the well. She feared that there might be poisonous creatures like snakes or scorpions hidden amidst the thick vegetation, because for them it was a safe sanctuary. There was nothing to threaten their existence. They might appear any moment and bite or sting her. What would she do if one such insect came out. The very thought of it sent a shudder down her spine.

She did not know when and how she could come out of this hell hole. Who would rescue her? But how would any one come here unless he had a reason to? And why should any one be coming this way? It was not a regular passage.......
There was hopelessness, wherever she looked. After a long wait, she got desperate. If no one came and pulled her out, she would die unseen and unheard. She also thought of her dear father: how much worried would he be. She thought she

must cry as loud as she could. She might be heard if she did so. But what if the cries went in vain? The thought of not being heard was a death to her. But that was the only way to be heard. She therefore, started giving out mighty cries after short intervals. It was a painful exercise, and caused pain in the throat. But it was a question of life and death….. If she was destined to die this way (how horrible it was), no body could save her. She was hanging perilously between hope and despair. Her efforts continued…………….

—————◆◆◆◆◆————

King Yayati found that in the chase of the quarry, he had come very far from his attendants. They were left miles behind. They must be looking for their king. Not all of them were on the horse back. Some were foot soldiers. Exhausted, he was feeling thirsty. From a distance he noticed the well of Devyani. It was his good luck, he thought, that he had notices it so easily. He turned his horse that way. As soon as Devyani sensed that there were tapping of the horse and they were heading towards her, her hopes reawakened. Some one was coming. And she resumed her cries for help. She knew if it was not now, then it would be never.

Yayati thought, he had heard a lady's cries for help. He looked around, but could see none. Was it an illusion? Sometimes our own senses play a game with us. Even the non existing objects appear visible, and the inaudible becomes audible. No, his senses were not playing a hide and seek. They were intact. The cry for help became clearer as he approached the well. He got curious. Coming to the well, he looked inside and found a girl sitting at the pit, looking helplessly towards the sky. He was amused and wondered how she was here. How could she fall into the well when its parapet was so high? Had she then jumped into it? But why should she? And if she had jumped on purpose, she would not make the world know about it. What ever be the circumstances, she had to be saved.

Seeing a stranger looking down into the well, Devyani was excited. God had sent her a saviour after all. He is so kind and great. She looked expectantly towards the onlooker, and signalled for taking her out. The king thought that it must have been an accident with her. The poor soul must have been desperate. Hardly ever a soul would pass this way. Any way, she had to be rescued. The well was fortunately not very deep. Years of neglect had invited some natural rubbish, and made it shallow. But how to pull her out? She could not be rescued by extending his hand, howsoever hard he tried. Suddenly he thought of the reins of his horse. Yes, they could be of great help. He scurried to the waiting creature, undid the knots of its reins and joining both of the reins lowered it. He had put a large knot at the end of the rope, so that one could easily hold on to it. The rope came to Devyani as a god-send. It was the proverbial 'lifeline'. Her joys knew no bounds. She was beside herself, when she saw the rope dangling before her. She looked towards the stranger as if to ask what to do. Their eyes exchanged their messages. She held on to the large knot precariously.

The object, the king was going to pull out of the well, was not an ordinary dead weight, but a human being. She had to be pulled out with due I care and tenderness. Any indiscretion could injure her. To ensure her safety, Yayati jumped on to the parapet, stood there and from there he started pulling the dame in distress. He could clearly notice the girl's expression of unease and fear, changing into one of relief and ecstasy as she came closer. She had got life after all. She was coming out of the mouth of hell. As she came up, the king lent his right hand for her help. She held it tightly, stood on the parapet and jumped out. He helped with his hands on her shoulders for managing herself. Her fall into the well and long, hopeless wait had visibly weakened her.

Now was Yayati able to look at her from head to foot. What a ravishing beauty, what charm, how beautifully chiselled! She was fit to be living in a king's palace. How come that such a bewitching girl was here!! And in this condition! He was face to face with her. He felt like owning her. But he could not be so vulgar. Can't she be an unearthly creature in the human form? He had heard so many stories in his childhood how ghosts and goblins transform themselves in human form and hunt them. But she might not be that! What made him opine so, he was not sure.

While the king was surveying the dame in distress and having thoughts about her, Devyani too was mystified by the royal bearing of the king. So muscular, so handsome, such a large chest and so kind at heart, so magnanimous! Otherwise who in this selfish world goes out of the way to help others? The person she was faced with, did not fit in the description of an ordinary man. His manners and decency showed his refined upbringing. All of a sudden she was reminded of her days with Kutch. It all came as a flash of lightning. He too was so handsome and likeable. But between the two, there was no comparison. He was a mere youth, this gentleman was a matured person who seemed to have seen the ways of the world. But why should she think of the past? It had devastated her and she had tried to obliterate its painful memories. This was not the time to spoil the present. That was not to come back, and this was in the hand.......

Both of them wished to know each other, who they were, what they did and from where they had come. Finding her naturally hesitant, the king said, "Who are you, young lady? What were you doing inside the well? What had happened to you? As for my self, I am Yayati, king of the neighbouring state. I had come for hunting a wild boar. Its chase brought me quite far from my attendants and retainers. Being hungry and thirsty I happened to be here to quench my thirst. In stead of quenching my thirst, I am standing before you. Now please tell me about yourself."

Devyani was dumb-founded. She was facing a king! And he had saved her! So he was her saviour and her protector. She was in a state of short trance. She found the king waiting for her reply. He should not be made to wait. "I am Devyani, the daughter of Guru Shukracharya, your excellency. We live in the ashram complex close to this place. I had come to the river bank for a bath with my neighbours. While returning, I got curious to know why people did not come to this well for water. I wanted to know what was actually wrong with it. For having a clear view of its inside, I climbed up to the parapet, and looked below. I cannot say, how I came to be here. Perhaps I had felt giddy and I stumbled. I had grown hopeless and lost the hope of rescue., because rarely people come this side. I am thankful to the Almighty and to your highness for the kind deed. Only by virtue of you sir, I have got another lease of life. You have given me life. I am too full of words to express my gratitude." And then she folded her hands in supplication.

"You need not say so many big things, dear lady. It was my duty to help you. What are human beings in this world for, if they don't cooperate and help each other? I am glad that you haven't sustained any injuries. We must thank the Almighty for that. It's getting late. People at your place must be waiting for you. Your absence must have made them worried. Come, I'll take you to your home. It's getting late. The sun down is not far away." Up till now they had come to the place where the horse stood. The king reined his beast again and invited her for a ride. In a trice she would be home. He mounted the beast himself first, and extended his hand for her to mount. The powerful hold of his hand for the pull gave her a thrill. She had a peculiar feeling that she needed this kind of hold. It was so reassuring!...... Soon they were home. He helped her dismount smoothly. She invited him to come to her modest abode. The king had no objection. She treated him to some choicest snacks. It was followed by a cool glass of water. The king thanked her profusely for her hospitality and was prepared to go.

"Where are you going, your majesty! You can't leave me behind. It is not done."

"What do you mean, young lady? Now that you have come home safe, it's time for me to go back. It's already late. I've a long way to go…... I could not get what you meant by saying "you can't leave me behind".

"Your honour, certainly you can't leave me behind. You are bound to me for ever."

This was the moment for Yayati to be puzzled. How was she 'bound' to him? One doesn't get bound to the other only by a chance meeting. People meeting at the public place do not get bound but soon part with the other.

He looked at her in amazement, as if asking her for a clarification.

Coming close to him, she quizzed, "Don't you know, your honour that only a husband can hold the hand of his wife? Now that you have held me by the hand, by virtue of the prevalent custom, you have become my hus –band and I, your spouse. You can't be so naive as not to be unaware of the prevalent customs." She was very emphatically persuasive in her tone.

"But my dear, Devyani. You could not be pulled out of the well without being held by my hand. Could you? It was a must for that moment. It was the need of the hour. You can't take it as your husband's hand. And as for me, I don't entertain any such notion about that. You need not accord undue significance to it."

"Well said, your excellency, well said. Please remember that committing a crime, even involuntarily, attracts the prescribed punishment. One could give the excuse that he never meant it, but it will not absolve him from the punishment. Isn't it, sir?"

"Yes, it's true. A crime is a crime after all whether committed intentionally or otherwise. But dear Devyani, you are stretching the matter rather too far. It doesn't merit that weightage. It is absolutely different."

Her arguments had some weight. Yayati was foxed for a moment. He must forward some other excuse to extricate himself from the net.

"Deavyani, do you know that in my palace I have several other queens. They are ok for me. And moreover, when you go there, you may find it uncomfortable to adjust there. There will be profusion of ill will and bad blood against you. And being the junior most, you will have to be subservient to them. That would be too humiliating. Being a married man, I should not go for another." Though he had tried to show his unwillingness to accept her as his next queen, at the core of his heart he had a keen desire to take her home. She would be the prettiest among his queens. She was a real gem, a person whom Lord Brahma had created with infinite patience and imagination on one of the days when he was at leisure. The king knew that whatever he had been trying to show, was mere farce. Wasn't he unusually lucky that such a heavenly beauty as her, was pressurizing him to marrying her? He could not have imagined of possessing a wife like her. And lo, she was coming to him on her own!

"But don't you think Devyani that your father may refuse his consent to this marriage?"

Devyani had noticed a thaw in the king's attitude. "Why do you think so, your honour?"

"Because marriages are made between persons of the same social status and caste. And we are different. You, a Brahman and I, a Kshatriya. Our customs don't permit their violation."

"Please don't worry no that count, sir. My father is a perfect gentleman and an indulgent father. He has always acted as per my wish—howsoever wild and impossible it might be. When he comes to know my desire to marry you, he will give his consent. He would never like to see his dear daughter in pain."

While the duo were talking the, sage came. He had never seen the stranger up till now. "Who is this Devi, and how come he is here?"

"Dear father, he is king Yayati. I am greatly obliged to him. He is my saviour and my protector. Had he not come to my aid, I would have been dead. You would not have seen my face. I would have died in your absence."

The sage was puzzled. What is his daughter saying? 'saviour and protector' 'death in my absence'? It was getting mysterious and intriguing.

"Were you in some sort of trouble, my dear? I never knew about it. What was it? Must have been life-threatening, dangerous? How did he come to be there? My dear, tell me. Through what sort of fire you had to pass and who caused it?"

"That I will relate, dear father in full detail. It is important. But more important is the question before us. That needs your attention."

"What's that, darling!"

"Honourable father, kindly permit me to be married to king Yayati. I am beholden to him for his kindness to me. He has given me another lease of life. I had been dead, but for him. And as he has given me this life, I wish to offer myself to him for ever. Don't I owe an obligation to him, father?"

Her father was stunned. How could this happen? Social customs did not sanction such a union. If the high and mighty in the society did not honour the social conventions, what will the ordinary people do? They follow their superiors' conduct. Brahmans were superior in the social hierarchy to the Kshatriyas. A superior could not stoop so low as to marry into the inferior's family. Of course, there were cases of exception in the past, but the exceptions are after all exceptions: not the rule. They are mere digressions.

He did not sanction. His reluctance was based on the social customs.

"But dear father, if I am to be wedded to any one, it is this man or no one. I shall remain unmarried for life."

The Guru was aware of his daughter's stubbornness. She would never give up. Her wishes had to be fulfilled. And for all this he was himself responsible. He had been pampering her since her childhood, as he did not want to see the apple of his eyes depressed for anything. Hadn't he revived Kutch both the times after the asuras had killed him? She had threatened on both the occasions that she would kill herself, if he were not brought to life. Where was the chance that she would follow his advice? She was rigid, he knew. He would have to do her bidding. Won't it be a family disgrace if she remained unmarried? A daughter has to be married and sent to her husband's house. He would be ridiculed and humiliated for not giving her away in marriage. People might say that the old man had not married her for his own comforts. He was too selfish and wanted her to stay with her so that she could look after him in his old age. No, he could not afford to listen to such unpalatable comments.

"My dear child, what you ask me to do is socially unacceptable. But for your pleasure, I shall have to make a compromise."

"I am sorry father for putting you in a tight situation, but this is a question of my life, my future. If I am not happy at the place of your choice, you would never forgive yourself, as you love me so deeply. I am aware of the customs and traditions, but there have been some departures in the past. Kindly let my case be also counted among those few. After all rules are made for the good of the people, not for their suffering. The departures in the past must have been made only due to the human consideration.

The sage found that his daughter was well versed in the worldly ways. She could not be easily prevailed upon. She had to be permitted. But for that he had to perform certain rituals. If a moment's displeasure was going to help matters and make the child's future happy, it was preferable. The unpleasantness will soon be a matter of the past and drowned into the ocean of future happiness.

The king was a mute witness to the things going on. He had seen how pliable the old man was. So much sacrificed for his daughter's well being! For her he could bend even the time-honoured customs!

Finding no way out of the puzzling situation, the Guru thought that it was better to succumb. Even otherwise, he would have to. But he must check with the king himself whether he was agreeable for the wedlock. Whether he was prepared to take her to the palace and accord his daughter her due importance. Because he was aware of kings having more than one spouses. He was concerned about her safety, security and her position. Yayati assured him that there was no reason to have such worries. Devyani would be accorded her due importance and would be at the top in the hierarchy. Yes, the wedlock was not in consonance of the prevailing social customs, but for the sake of her happiness and future, an exception could me made. The sage was competent for overruling the convention. Because it is only the high ups and wise men like him, that give direction to the society. Their decision could not be questioned. Now it was entirely up to the sage to do as he wished.

Guru Shukracharya had got the answers to his doubts. The king had not only given his consent but also guaranteed her elevated position in the palace. If he were even the least bit unwilling, it would have shown in his reply. The sage was glad that his daughter was going to a place, a match which he could have never provided. Her social status was going to be higher than girls like her generally deserved. In view of her bright future, bending of the social customs was not undesirable. After all, the greatest good of a person should be the outlook of a system.

The Guru therefore, gave his consent after the deliberation. Devyani was beside herself with joy. She knew that her father, though a stickler for discipline, would make an exception in her case. He could not imagine of hurting her feelings even though it were overtly improper. His weakness for her always made him lose.

By this time the king's attendants and retainers, who had been left behind in the chase had reached the Guru's ashram. They could feel their arrival by the shuffling of their feet and the commotion. It was the time for the king to return. In view of the pressing circumstances, the Guru took the duo to the 'puja room' and performed the rituals of their wedlock. With his vast learning and time-honoured pedantry, who could be a better priest than the Guru himself! He was more particular about the solemn oath taken by the duo for mutual understanding, fidelity and their respect for each other. At the conclusion of the ceremony, the duo touched his feet and sought his blessings for a happy life.

As things had got naturally delayed, the Guru did not allow the king to leave for the palace so late at night. It was proper to spend the night here in the ashram. The attendants and the retainers who had come in search of their master, were also advised to make themselves comfortable in the open courtyard. As for their meals, they always carried sufficient provision for the team when out on a hunting expedition.

Yayati made it known to the Guru that he would not be taking away Devyani with him this time. As a queen, she deserved due formalities. Therefore, on one of the coming auspicious days, he would be arriving here with a royal entourage for carrying the new queen to the palace. The proposal found favour both with father and his daughter. After all there were certain formalities to be observed for such an occasion.

After the blissful stay for the night, the king left the ashram next morning. Devyani earnestly desired to go with her man, it was impossible to live without him. But she saw reason in what the king had said. Sometimes she feared the king might forget about her throwing his promises to the wind. But soon she consoled herself that it was not to be. The intensity with which both loved each other could not be falsified. He would certainly make his promise of taking her to the palace good.

5

The Untold Story

G URU SHUKRACHARYA WAS GLAD THAT his daughter had got
the man of her dream. She would be happy now. The
greater news was that she would be the consort of a king.
Her ashram friends would be jealous of her lot.

What ever the gods have willed, happens. Even the
impossible becomes possible. Yes, there were customary
hurdles, but they had been overcome by virtue of the
authority vested in (wise men like) him.

But he was curious to know about the circumstances
in which Devi had met the king. Why did she call him her
'saviour' and 'protector'? How could he give her another life?
There must have been a dangerous situation from which the
king had rescued her. What was that? And how had it come
about? He must ask her to narrate it in full……. So many
things had happened in his absence and he did not know! It
was nothing short of a disgrace for a girl's father.

His curiosity to learn the things from her took him to her
room, but she was sound asleep. He let her sleep. She had

had a stormy weather yesterday. God knows what sort of ugliness she had to face. He thought of talking about it in the evening, after he was back from the court and had finished with his evening prayers.

Devi looked fresh in the evening. This was the time to broach the subject. But he needed a little more time to finish with his rituals. As soon as he was free, he called her. She knew it was the time for her father to have a refreshing drink and talk to each other. She prepared the concoction for him and took it to him. He looked into her eyes. They were glistening and sharp. Right moment to ask. "Devi, did you have an accident yesterday?"

"Yes father, I had fallen into the old, blind well."

"But how could it be, dear? Its parapet is not on the ground level but sufficiently high, so that animals grazing in the field might not stumble into it. How could you fall into it then? Were you sitting on parapet? Were you too tired? If it was so, it is not the place to sit. Were you all by yourself or any one with you?"

Her father had shot so many questions at her. He wanted to go to the bottom of the case. Because the case was extraordinary. Had the king not rescued her, she might have died there. He must have lost her forever.

She was in a quandary whether she should narrate everything happening between her and Sharmistha. But she decided that she must. That quarrelsome rascal and arrogant princess had to be punished and made to pay for her misdeeds.

She started thus, "Dear father, both me and Sharmistha had a plan to celebrate the festival of spring together. As per plan, she came to our ashram along with her attendant, who was carrying her new clothes for the occasion. First of all we went out and collected a huge amount of flowers for weaving our ornaments. After coming home, we prepared several trinkets for us and left for the river bath. While we were enjoying our games in the river, there came a sudden storm. We thought of rushing out for the bank, but we waited for a while. Then the storm weakened and stopped. But it had done us a lot of harm. It had mixed up our clothes: they got entangled with each other.

"I felt cold and was shivering. It was mostly because of the wind. I asked my friend to come out as I was going out. But she did not. She wanted to enjoy the water-sport a little longer with other girls. When I came to the bank, I found our clothes in a lump. As both of us had got the sets of similar hue and design, I could not distinguish between mine and hers, and I put on her clothes in confusion. After I had finished putting on the clothes, she came out of the water with hurried steps. She stumbled by mistake and sprained her leg. She was in pain. But before I could rush for her help, she had come with the support of an ashram girl, limping. I was sorry for her lot.

"Her pain had made her irritable and cross. When she noticed me, glittering in the new finery, she lost temper. Her painful walk had made her cross and irritable. She shrieked, "You rascal, you had the audacity to put on my clothes! Couldn't you distinguish between your shoddy stuff and my magnificent make!" I pleaded ignorance, but she was getting abusive. She said that I had willfully put on her clothes, a set which my father could never purchase. How could he? He was just a poor employee of her father, the king. The reason of my putting on the dress was that even if I had taken off her set to return it, she would not put it on. It was below her dignity to put on a used set. Consequently, I would be putting on that set in future. In her opinion it was my devious plan. She further added that coming from a poor and disadvantaged family, no better conduct could be expected from me. All this while, we were walking back to the ashram. By the time we had come near the well, she was obviously very tired. She needed rest. Despite my being hurt, I helped her perch on to the parapet. There too, more insulting words followed. She would stop at nothing. She had made up her mind to thoroughly humiliate me. Being enraged, she stood up, slapped me and pushed me violently into the well.

"I lay crying for help in the well for quite some time. I was sure to die there. And because the well doesn't lie on the regular path, there was no chance of anyone passing that way, hence no one hearing me cry for help. By my good luck, king Yayati happened to come there in course of chasing a quarry. He was hungry and thirsty. The well had attracted him. He never knew that it was a dry one. Hearing my painful cries for help, he first ensured who was inside the pit and then managed to pull me out with the help of his horse's reins.

"Father, this is the height of insulting conduct. She had not only passed demeaning remarks against you, she had also the audacity to call us beggars and made a murderous attempt to kill me. What would you have done without me, father! Father, it's not only that the princess holds us in light esteem, this is the popular sentiment amongst the asuras. Why don't you remember that it were these people, who had killed the poor Kutch twice. It was only by virtue of your power of 'Sanjeevavni' that you had revived him both the times. Actually we are all despised, we are hated for being Brahmans and Aryans. Father dear, it is not advisable to live and work at a place where neither there is respect nor there is guarantee of life. We cannot live under the shade of terror and threat to life. I urge you upon my bended knees to listen to me and move some where, where we are recognized and respected for our worth."

It was a sad tale of audacity, jealousy, hatred, ill will and insult. It also showed that attempt on their life could also be made whenever the palace wanted. Devi was right. The princess's conduct was indicative of the general sentiment of the people in the palace. Of course, the king was very respectful to him personally, and there was a great rapport between them, but all this was perhaps a sham. He had to do so, as he wanted to keep him in good humour. He was invaluable for the whole asura race. Without him their survival was at stake.

Devyani knew that her father was too gentle to tell the king that he was not ready to live here, and that the general climate in the kingdom was one of hostility towards them. Devyani had doubts about the success of her pleadings with him. Her ire against Sharmistha would not let her take rest. It would be smouldering as long as she was here. She must pressurize her dear father to leave this place immediately. Every single moment was painful to her, as it would always remind her of the abuses and insults hurled by that spiteful girl, on her and her father. When she felt that her father looked hesitant, she declared that she would fast unto death if he did not tell the king about his decision to leave this place.

<hr/>

The Guru was terribly upset. But for peace at home, he had to talk to the king. He just could not run away from the kingdom without any intimation. That would be disgraceful. He approached the king at a proper juncture. He posted him with his desire to leave his kingdom and go elsewhere, where he would get both recognition and security to life. The Guru's words felt like molten glass in his ears. What is the Guru saying? If he goes, everything would be lost. On him depended the future victories of his army in any battle whatsoever. What had happened to the Guru?, the king wondered. It must have been very serious and unearthly.

The sage was not a shallow person. If he had made up his mind, he must have done it after due consideration. Circumstances must have compelled him to take recourse to this extreme step. First of all, he must ask the Guru what ails him and why he was prepared to take such an extreme step.

"Guruji, why have you taken such a decision all of a sudden? Never did you voice your problems or your discomfort. Had there been any thing wrong, and had I come to know of it, it would have been righted. Any way, I beg of you to kindly tell me your difficulties," the king was standing before him with folded hands.

"Dear Vrish, You have known me since long. I never wanted to bring frivolous matters before you. That would have been wasting your valuable time. You have got hundreds of things to attend to. Of course, there were serious problems before me, but I managed to deal with them at my own level. But now I think I should have brought them to your kind notice. Actually ignoring them gave out a wrong signal to the mischief makers."

The king wondered why his spies kept him in the dark up till now. It is really a matter of great concern that something disturbing happens to the royal mentor and advisor, and that is not reported. The Guru had every reason to believe that all the mischiefs were committed within the king's knowledge.

The king prayed to the Guru to be more specific and give instances of the mischiefs. The king's intention was to learn how grave they were. The seriousness of a crime was to be the yardstick of its impact on the Guru.

Now Shukracharya had to show how he had been put to terrible inconvenience. He said that on two occasions, his friend Brihaspati's son Kutch, who had come to him to study at his feet, had been done to death by a handful of unknown assailants. The boy's savage killing was a personal loss to him personally, because he was the son of his bosom friend. The boy's safety and security was his personal responsibility. With what face could he explain his murder to his friend? But by virtue of his knowledge of 'Sanjeevani', he had revived him. It was certainly shocking that the king had no information of both the killings. As a matter of fact the whole of the capital city knew it. In such circumstances, any one could think that these killings had the blessings of the king. He (the sage) had tolerated them and had carried on as usual. He had never made it an issue with the court. Because if the king was already aware of the 'deeds', what was the use of bringing it to his notice? And even if it was brought, he would have advanced some lame excuses viz, the failure of the system, and assured him of punishing the criminals.

Vrishparva's face showed that he was visibly disturbed and feeling embarrassed. He thought that the Guru had had his say. But it was not the end. 'What would he say more', the king thought.

"The matter doesn't end here only, 0 king. Yesterday's incident has badly shaken me. I'm sure you are aware of it."

"No, Guruji, I'm not aware of any incident to tell you the truth. Kindly tell me what happened. How are these things happening one after another, and I am kept in darkness!"

"Dear Vrish, your daughter Sharmistha had gone to the river bank with Devyani for a bath yesterday. While returning home, there was a quarrel between them over the abusive words used by your daughter, both for me and Devyani. She had taunted against my social status and my employment vis-à-vis your royal status. My daughter naturally protested. The matter precipitated. They grew physical. In a fit of uncontrollable rage your daughter pushed Devyani into a well, and ran away from there. My poor child kept on crying for help for long. But no one heard, because the well is not along the regular path. Rarely people pass by that way. By her good luck, a thirsty stranger happened to pass by that way. He heard her cry as he came to the well and rescued her.

Yesterday's incident has badly hurt my poor child. It was a murderous attempt on her life, like the attempts made upon my friend's son, your honour. All these acts have confirmed our fears that we are neither welcome here nor are we safe. There seems to be a general hostility towards us. I had taken a lighter view of the previous happenings, but the recent event has traumatized her. She is not ready to stay here even for a moment and is fasting herself to death to compel me to leave this place immediately. Considering her plight, I am also compelled to take this decision. I have tried to share my inner feelings with you, so that your honour might not take my decision as rash and undesirable. I had to subscribe to my daughter's view after viewing the things in their proper background.

O king, as things stand, I cannot let my daughter die. She is my life and my purpose for living. There is nothing for me if she be not there. We are going away the next morning."

The king was both stunned and stupefied. The world seemed to be coming to an end for him. The sage was a great support for their whole race. Their future revolved around him. Through him they got strength. Such unpleasant things had happened, and he was ignorant! It was criminal! If the sage had come to such a conclusion, he was fully justified: there was nothing wrong in it. Any one in his place would have thought like that. It is a credit that he had not bothered me with his problems in the previous two murder cases. He was graceful enough not to worry me but deal the matter himself. Although by any standard, these were the cases of law and order: Assassination of the Guru's ward by our own residents? How shameful!!

"Guruji, I am deeply ashamed for whatever had happened to you and your daughter. I am also deeply pained to learn of these horrible acts. I just don't know how to beg of you to pardon me. I don't think I have a face for it. I cannot but beg of you to change your decision of leaving this place. We cannot think of living without you. Guruji, kindly revise your decision."

"O.K. Vrish, did your daughter not tell you any thing about her quarrel with my daughter? Because as you claim, you had no information about any event. But how could it be so?"

"Yes Gurudeva, I swear that she has not even breathed about her such a dastardly act. Yes, she was unusually quiet and avoided mixing up with people yesterday, but both me and my dear wife thought it to be one of her mood swings. In adolescence, as the children grow, they have their own fantasies and yearnings. She might have been cross on account of that. We tried to speak to her but she was reticent. We left it to herself, thinking that she would soon come to normalcy.

I really wonder why she should have pushed her bosom friend into a well. That was monstrous and not pardonable. You are right that Devyani might have died in the pit unseen and unknown. I really thank the gentleman who had saved us from such a devastation. I shudder to think of a person, dying in a well for want of timely rescue. God be thanked for His Grace.

King Vrish was puzzled what to do. How to mollify the Guru and his daughter? As a matter of fact, the Guru could be managed somehow or the other. He was a perfect gentleman, very easily pliable. 'The real rub lay with his daughter. She had been grievously hurt by the act of his daughter. She was adamant to leave the city and had urged her father to shift. The Guru would do, whatever she commanded. So the most important thing was to manage her whatever be the cost. Because, on her depended the continuance of the Guru in his court and the future of his race.

Looking helpless with a pathetic expression, he asked the Guru, "What is your order, Guruji? Do you want us to be destroyed in the coming years? You are the Life to us. Without you there's none. On behalf of the people of the land I pray to you to change your decision." The king noticed an obvious thaw in the Guru. He knew that his prayers and supplications won't go unrewarded. He was relieved. Now half the battle had been won.

"All right Vrish. I never meant any harm to you or the people. I am moved by your prayers and am inclined to change my decision. You really don't appear to be involved. But the problem lies with Devyani. If you wish everything to be well, you will have to win over her. You have to please her at any cost. If not, I cannot help you."

"I'll be doing what she wants me to do, honourable Guruji. After all she is like my daughter. Several times have we met each other in the palace, when she was playing with Sharmistha. On the basis of our rapport and my position as her uncle, she should be honouring my wishes."

"I think so, 0 king. I wish you well. She must listen to you. After all you are the ruler of the land. It is something great that the king himself is requesting some one so young to honour his bidding."

"All right, Guruji, I want to see her myself and talk to her. I wish to see what has hurt her most. I shall try to find out a solution. No problem in the world is such that it can't be solved. Please tell her about my visit, sir."

"As you wish, O king. You are most welcome to our modest abode."

It was proper for the king to see his own daughter before visiting her victim, and gauge the seriousness of the problem. What had actually happened that had enraged her so much that she had pushed her friend into the well? Who was at fault? Who had instigated whom? By any standard, Sharmistha should not have pushed her into the well. It was monstrous. The poor girl would have died there unattended. His daughter had her own version of the story. But the crux of the matter was the push. Sharmistha felt sorry and admitted that her act was too rash, but in her rage she did not foresee the outcome. She also admitted that she should have informed either of her parents about her deed, so that they could arrange for her rescue. It was unpardonable not to inform them. When looked into the background, she now realized what a blunder she had committed in her anger. It could have proved fatal. Both of her parents reprimanded her for her rashness and indiscretion.

The king further informed his family that if the Guru and his daughter were not mollified, they could leave their country for another land. There was no dearth of people who could provide him patronage. He also said that Devyani was the prime mover in the family and controlled her father. The poor man was too indulgent to displease her over any thing. As she was adamant, she was a hard nut to crack. But she had to be pleased at every cost. God knows, how low he would have to stoop before her. It was very humiliating for him. Playing to the tunes of a pampered child was not easy, and the result thereof could not be forecast.

6

A Shameful Term for Peace

KING VRISHPARVA WAS SEEN COMING to the ashram. He stopped his horse a little away from the cottage and got down. His attendants following him took charge of the steed. The Guru came out of his verandah and welcomed the royal visitor. After the exchange of normal greetings, the king desired to be taken to the girl. And now he was in the inner chamber. The girl was seated on the sparsely cushioned bed. Although the king had entered the room with his Guru, she looked indifferent. The king was not used to such indifference and disrespect. He felt ruffled, but it was not the occasion to show his displeasure. He had to be practical. It was altogether a different matter. It was related to emotional turbulence. It needed a sensitive handling. One's ego had no place in it.

For a few moments he looked intently at Devyani, then asked, "Hellow my dear, how are you? I have learnt that you are in a great fury. The place where you have lived so long does not have any charm for you? "It made no difference in her expression. He came closer and held one of her hands, lying limp by her side and said, "My dear Devi, have you forgotten your dear uncle so soon? Making no response to him? See, I have come all the way from the palace, just to see you and ask why you are so disturbed." The girl looked into his affectionate eyes and tried to smile.

"Come on, my darling, tell me why you are displeased with us. I suppose your friend Sharmistha had hurt you. I did not know about yesterday's accident. I learnt of it through honourable Guruji. It has badly upset me. But I knew that it had upset you the more. My dear, both of you were friends for such a long time. You have been together through thick and thin. Being more intelligent and matured than her, I request you to pardon her. I have heavily reprimanded her for being rash and indiscreet with her own friend. She was herself horrified at what she had done, in a fit of uncontrollable rage. She says that she has no face to come to you, and ask for forgiveness.

"Granted that her act was unpardonable and it could have cost your life, but it was a result of momentary madness. Let the bonds of your relations not snap only due to an act of foolishness. Is it o.k.?"

But her bitterness was not to be softened by the affectionate words of the king. She was not ready to accept his words and offer to forgive and forget her tormentor. She had made up her mind not to make friends with her again. How could one be friendly again with one who had tried to kill her?

Didn't Sharmistha know that I would die in the well? That there was no chance of any body ever passing through that way? And if nobody would pass by that way, I was sure to die. No, peace cannot be made with her. She would always remain an eye sore for her.

The king was greatly perturbed as the girl would not speak. Her rigidity was nauseating and insurmountable. What would be the result of her not coming to our terms? We shall lose her father's secret powers and would be as much vulnerable to attacks as we had been. No, that situation had to be saved. But how? That was the question. The girl was not prepared to listen to any word of advice. Her only 'slogan' was not to stay here at any cost. But that could not be allowed to happen. The king felt like standing before a mightier power before whom he had to surrender. It was so disgusting! But he had no other option. He felt humiliated, but for the good of his people he had to gulp whatever indignities were to come. He could not afford to react. That would be disastrous. He tried to approach the stubborn creature again.

"My dear, none of us wants you to leave us and go elsewhere. We have lived here so well and peacefully till now. What will the people say? That we could not adjust, and fell apart. That would bring a bad name." Then with a bated breath he uttered, "Now what we are going to say to each other is only between you and us. The world would never smell of it. I am ready to fulfill every condition you make. Say whatever you wish. I have to do it because you are not agreeable and are bent upon leaving. But we don't want to lose you." This was the maximum the king could stoop.

"Honourable sir, (she could have addressed him as 'uncle' as the kind had addressed her as his child), I have heard you. But my oath to leave this place, which has been triggered by the series of onslaughts and humiliations on us and lastly on me personally, cannot be changed. I am clear about it."

Her words of anger were a great blow to the king's attempts to win her. The girl is totally spoilt by her father and knows not what to speak and to whom. Where are her family 'sanskaras' gone? She is completely oblivious even of the common courtesies. There was a desperation in the air. It was just like losing a battle, but as a fighter ruler he did not want to lose. Nothing in this world is impossible. There is always a way out –whether noble or ignoble.

"All right, dear. Supposing what you are saying is correct and final, do you think anything else could be done to please you, and make you agreeable to stay?" Her father who was also present in the room, was getting fidgety. It was highly embarrassing to see his daughter behave so indifferently with the king. It was the height of impertinence. Really, she had thrown her family 'sanskaras' to the wind. What would the king feel about him? He wanted to intervene, but it was not right.

The king was waiting impatiently for her response. Her silence was telling upon his nerves. Seconds seemed to be hours. Ultimately she opened her mouth. "Sir, there is absolutely no question of my reunion with your daughter, Sharmistha. I cannot stand her even in my dreams.....I am agreeable to stay with my father only on one condition that Sharmistha is made to work as my slave. When I am married and go to my husband's place, she would also follow me there as my personal attendant. It would be service for life. Nothing more or nothing less than that." Saying these words she looked at the king.

Her words were like bombshells to the ears of both of them. What was the girl saying? Is she in her senses? Such a condition is bizarre and unearthly. Who had ever heard of a sage's daughter asking for the king's daughter to work under her like her slave!! It was not only wicked, mean-minded but blatantly demeaning. They were still not able to believe that the girl in the corner had made such an impossible demand. She must have been crazy to utter so. The king was tongue-tied. He was shocked beyond measure. Did he have to make such a sacrifice for his land? His daughter who had been bred and brought up in the luxury of the palace was to become the slave of a mere sage's daughter!! It was just unthinkable and inconceivable. He found he had nothing more to say to the girl. She had delivered her verdict. It was for the listeners to comply.

Grave disappointment was writ on the king's countenance. He was dazed and speechless. Now the question was what to be done. How could he break the news to his queen? She would be as devastated as him.

The Guru was saddened by whatever had happened with the king. He wanted to know from his daughter, why she had put such an ugly condition before him. It was shameful and demeaning. At this she replied that her condition was a double-edged weapon. If the king disapproved, then they would be leaving this kingdom, and if not, his daughter will have to pay for her mischief for the whole life. The Guru was further saddened by the meanness of his daughter. From where had she got such an idea of revenge! Had one ever heard of a princess becoming the slave of an ordinary girl! But he knew that she would have her way. They would have to wait for the signal from the palace about the decision.

King Vrishparva found it difficult to broach the matter before his queen. How shell-shocked she would be? Her daughter, the princess becoming a slave to the Brahman's girl, the man who was her master's ordinary employee like many others!! And when the king talked to her, her reactions were the same as he had expected. He had a difficult time persuading her to accept the verdict. It was for the good of their whole race. There had been instances in the past when for the sake of common good, one life was sacrificed. It was considered a pious offering at the altar of the mother earth.

The queen had to condescend with a heavy heart. She wondered what kind of life would the poor girl be made to live, after she had become her friend's slave. The wicked girl would certainly make her life difficult. It would be nothing short of torture-- a living death. But what could be done, if she was destined to suffer. There is no fight against Destiny. One had to suffer it. What cannot be cured, must be endured.

Two hurdles had been crossed: the king and the queen. They had resigned to their fate. Parents can only give birth to a child. They cannot govern its future. It has to face what has been determined by God. It was dictated by its deeds in the previous birth. So though the girl was born in the royal family, her destiny will take her where she had to go. There is no other way.

The third hurdle was to convince the princess of the shocking verdict. As was expected, Sharmistha never expected that her 'one time friend' would be so mean and stoop so low as to compel her parents to give her as a slave to her enemy. But both the king and the queen convinced that her sacrifice was a guarantee for the safety and security of the whole of the asura race. On her decision depended the lot of the future generations. So many people in the past have sacrificed their lives for the common cause. And the society worships them as their heroes. They become immortals. Such a lot had fallen to her. It was a momentous occasion. Granted that her life would be completely transformed, but she had to accept that this was the way destiny had decided for her.

The very thought of serving her wicked, revengeful and vicious friend frightened her beyond measures. She was horrified at the thought of serving her. But she later compromised with the circumstances. Weren't her parents sad? But being helpless, they could not ward it off. She should not think only of her comforts, she had to think of the future generations of her race. Would she like them to be decimated, and no trace left of them? O, that would be disastrous! The future generations would curse her for her selfishness. Thinking thus, she ultimately gave in. She told her parents that she was prepared to accept her lot. One must not lose hope in the future. Things might get better. Who knows Gods would be kind to her!

Her parents had a sigh of relief. But they were remorseful and guilt-stricken. They were going to sacrifice their dear daughter before their very eyes. Wasn't it selfish of them? Themselves they would be rolling in wealth and comforts in the palace, while their daughter would be slogging at the hands of her vicious tormentor. But they too compromised soon. What else could they do? This is what had to be............

The decision was conveyed to the ashram through a reliable messenger. It pleased one but disturbed the other. The sage was pained to hear a devilish laughter emanating from his daughter's room.

7

Another Queen in the Palace

KING YAYATI ARRIVED AT THE ashram with a huge procession of horses, elephants, camels shining in their glittering outfits. He had to wait for the auspicious day as advised by the royal astrologers and priests. After their return to the palace, the marriage was to be performed again with all the formalities. Guru Shukrachrya sent his daughter to her new abode. Whatsoever it be, she was after all the light of this house. He would have no life without her. What other interest was left in this life without her? But soon he compromised with himself. Was he the only father giving away his daughter to another man? This is the way devised by the seers of the past. This thought gave him solace. Now he had to learn to live without her. For that matter, which father had ever kept his daughter with himself for life!!

Special arrangement was also made to carry Sharmistha with the returning marriage party.

Devyani was accorded the royal welcome she deserved. The king accorded her the highest status in the hierarchy which was not liked by the previous queens. But it was the desire of the king, therefore there was no problem. Devyani soon adjusted to the life style of the passage. Things were not as strange for her, because she had often visited the royal apartments at the previous station and was familiar with the aristocratic ways.

The king had got an inkling of the bitter relationship of his spouse with her attendant. He sometimes wondered at the things. But did not discuss it. But he pitied her attendant's lot. He did not appreciate her harsh and subhuman treatment by his new wife., but let the things go as they did. Sharmistha was provided accommodation outside the royal apartments, along with those of the palace servants and attendants. These apartments were certainly on the palace premises, but they were at the farther end along the periphery.

Devyani derived a devilish pleasure in torturing her 'bosom friend' and often taunted for her inability in carrying out a menial job. She saw that she was always on her toes, hardly getting a breathing space. The poor soul had never toiled so much in her life. But there was no use cursing her fate. That life, lived till now, was a thing of the past and carried no meaning. Thinking of those palace days pained her. She was gradually learning to accept the life. The only saving grace for her was the softness shown to her by the king himself. Such a gesture of the highest worked as a soothing balm to her injured feelings. She felt that the king sympathized with her because of her previous background. But he could not dare doing anything concrete for fear of her rival.

Life flowed on its natural way. Days rolled into weeks, weeks into months and months into years. The strained relations between the 'once friends' remained unchanged. Devyani's feelings of hatred and anger for Sharmistha was as acute as it initially was. In course of time it should have shown some remission, but unfortunately, it had not. It was rather unnatural. But that was the way she was made.

Whenever the king wanted to relax, he would come down to the vast expanse of the green on the palace premises. The green trees swaying in the breeze, their fruits, the flowering plants emanating different flavours worked as a soothing balm to his troubled soul. Sometimes his queens too accompanied him. Devyani was not a regular visitor. The palace life interested her more. She found pleasure in various items of luxury. Where was the time for an evening walk? It was a cumbersome thing: a self-inflicted punishment. It was irrelevant. When urged persuasively by her favourite handmaids, who swore that the nature looked outside really captivating, she would come to the green and oblige them. But she realized that they were really correct. However, such visits were few and far between. Years had to wait for this favour by the new queen.

8

An Avoidable Disaster

D EVYANI COULD NOT RECOLLECT WHEN she had come last to this part of the apartments, meant for the palace attendants and servants. Actually she had an utter disdain for these low grade people. Their very sight caused repulsion in her. But as the queen she should also have taken care of the people serving her. It would be a grand gesture and encouraging for them. They would think that their masters too had a soft corner in their heart. And it was a sort of reward for them. As a matter of fact there was no need for masters to visit this area, but it had its own significance.

While the apartment –dwellers were busy with their domestic chores inside, their kids were playing in the open. Among the kids playing in the garden, Deavyani noticed two, who attracted her attention. They did not look ordinary, but different from the whole lot. Their body structure, their large eyes, their curling hair, and their broad forehead showed that they were not the menials' kids. She felt they resembled her own kids so much. She was curious to know about their identity. She asked her royal maid to go to them and bring them to her. After they had come, the maid was signalled to get away from there.

The kids were curious. Why had the queen sent for them? What did she want to ask?

"What's your names, kids?" she asked them affectionately. She wanted them to feel comfortable. The fear of talking to a queen need not be there. It might make them stiff and formal.

"Puru and Aayu" they replied together as if in a chorus. They were still holding each other's hands and swinging them.

"O, I see. Your names are very sweet and very interesting. Where do you live kids?"

"Over there, your highness. They were pointing to a modest dwelling in the distance. Devyani tried to see it.

"Who lives with you, dear?"

"We live with our mother, madam."

"Do you know her name, kids? If you know, can you tell me? I would very much like to meet her."

"Meet our mother, madam!! All right. We shall take you there. Her name is Sharmistha".

"O Sharmiatha! that's your mother's name?"

"Yes, ma'm."

"All right, take me there." and they started for the house. on the way she asked them again, "Who is your father, kids?"

"We don't know, ma'm."

"He lives here with you or some where else, in another city?"

"No ma'm, he lives in this palace."

"How do you know that he lives in this palace?"

"Because whenever he comes here, he says that he is very busy. He has no time to enjoy his life. He cannot go out whenever he wishes."

"I see, must be a busy person then. Have you seen him?"

"Yes, ma'm. He is fair, tall, with large eyes, flowing curls, muscular body and a large chest. Sometimes we used to climb on his shoulders and ran our fingers through his hair. It is very soft."

The kids' description of their father had made her suspicious. Their description matched with her husband—Yayati. Her worst fears seemed to be coming true. Was that man playing a double game with her? Did he have an illicit relation with Sharmistha? Were these children through him? They look so much like her own two sons! But she shrugged herself. She did not want to believe it. She should not rush to a conclusion without checking the things herself. She must verify the things with Sharmistha.

In the mean time they had come to the house. The door was closed. The kids were very excited that the queen herself had come to their house. They knocked at the door repeatedly. They wanted their mother to see the royal guest. What a surprise it would be for her! Their little hearts were jumping and dancing with joy.

"Sharmisrha! how are you?", asked the visitor with astonishment.

It was Sharmistha'a turn to be surprised. How could she come here! But she tried her best to look calm and normal. She thought that if Devyani needed her services urgently, she could have sent for her through a messenger and she would have gone. What was the purpose of coming here?

"I'm fine, your highness. Any urgent situation? You could have called me to the palace. Why take the trouble to come so far?" she replied.

Perhaps Devyani did not hear her words. She was too full of rage to say anything. She did not want to waste either time or words. Without giving any clarification for the visit, she shot at her, "Sharmistha, are these your children?"

"Yes they are mine, madam."

"But you're not married! How could you bear children?"

"Madam, this question is too personal to answer. It is a matter related to me. I am not obliged to answer it."

"How dare you say that it is a personal matter? You are living on the palace premises. I am responsible for the lives and property of my people and their activities too. You are one of our staff. If you are going to have children out of wedlock, what impact will it have on the character of the people here! I cannot allow immoral and unethical activities here. You can't be allowed to live the way you wish. You have to follow the social norms. Right?"

Sharmistha was speechless at the sudden flurry of allegations and the outburst. How as she going to answer her foe?

Devyani repeated her query again, "Sharmistha, I demand to know, how could you get children without marriage? You will have to explain and satisfy me. Do it just now."

Sharmistha knew it well how nasty Devyani could be and how low could she stoop. But if Devyani was not going to spare her, why should she not shake her by telling her the monstrous truth? If she had the wickedness to reduce her to this state of drudgery and slavery, she could also reply her in the same fashion. For a moment she forgot that she was the employee of Devyani and was bound to serve her unquestionably. She seemed to have regained the original self of a proud princess and the daughter of king Vrishparva.

"All right Devyani, then be prepared to hear the blasted truth. Steel yourself for that..... These kids of mine are through the man I love and adore, the man who is of my caste and my social status!"

"His name?"

"Yayati."

It was another bolt from the blue. So the truth, she had feared had ultimately come true. But how was Sharmistha to be squarely blamed for all this? Her own man had been cheating her and had indulged in a secret liaison with this woman. It also meant that as the king's better half, she herself had failed to bind her man, and he had to look at the greener pasture. The thought of some deficiency in her own self disturbed her. That had been capitalized by this woman. She was further enraged by the feeling of inferiority to her enemy.

"Sharmistha, it is not only shameful but disgusting. Didn't you know that he is my husband and that I had the sole right over him? Didn't you know that we had entered into a sacred wedlock before the fire god? But you had no qualms in cheating another woman!! You had the audacity to establish an illicit relationship with her husband!! Shame on you for what you have done! You have ruined me."

"Devyani, I have heard with patience what all you had to say. But in my opinion you are the person, who has to be ashamed of herself for what ever she has done. You are the daughter of a Brahman sage. By virtue of that you should have married a Brahman boy, not a Kshatriya. I am qualified for such a marriage because of being a Kshatriya king's daughter. But you transgressed the social limits. Your poor father was unwilling for your wedlock but compelled by you, he had to give in and go against the social norms. He knew that you would never listen to any body.

"As for my liaison with the king, I don't have any qualms about it. I have had relationship with a man of my caste and my status. As a matter of fact he is more of mine than yours. Even the holy books prescribe such a relationship. These books permit a woman to go to a man of her choice if she feels the need of it. Therefore, I have done what the books say. It's you who have done the reverse."

There was nothing wrong in what Sharmistha had said. She was on the right side of the law. But the truth always hurts and disturbs. Devyani had lost her argument. Her rival had blunted the sharpness of her weapon. Granted that she had done something illegal, but was it not true that her husband too had played her false? He was no epitome of virtues either.

Devyani was feeling terribly upset: she was defeated by her own rival, whom she had made a slave out of hatred. But here she had scored over her. She had the upper hand. Devyani wanted to give vent to her anger and defeat, she wanted to shout at someone, but she did not know what to do and whom to punish. He was not here. Being mad with anger and ready to burst, she looked here and there. It was lucky that she had asked her royal maid to get away and the kids had been asked to go and play outside. They should not have witnessed the ugly scene.

Devyani returned to the palace feeling lost and devastated. She took her man to task for his extra marital adventures. But a king could have some concubines. What was wrong and unusual about that? But here the hurtful thing was that her rival was his concubine. She had stolen his affection over her. This is what was more painful to her ego. She felt awfully downgraded. It was the defeat of her womanhood. Defeat of a woman whose beauty and charms were talked about far and wide, and of which she was unduly conceited.

Yayati laughed away her tantrums, saying it was one the king's privileges. Since time immemorial such things had been happening. No queen worth the name had ever questioned it. Why should she be worried over this? This was no issue. It was irrelevant. But her flame could not be doused by quoting the customs and conventions. Had it been the case with with some other woman, she would not mind it. But this case was totally different. It was the case of her rival scoring over her. It had proved that her husband her greater fascination for that woman. In other words she was dearer to him. It was unpalatable and therefore, could not be digested. Her restlessness knew no end. She must go to her father and complain against her husband's act of indiscretion. For her, only the old man could do justice. She felt she would know no peace unless justice was done in the case. And justice meant punishment for being willfully errant and deviant.

Guru Shukracharya had just finished his morning puja and meditation. Things were going at a slower pace in the ashram now. He had to manage the things of daily needs himself. So where was the hurry? He was surprised to see a royal chariot enter his courtyard with some horsemen in attendance. He stayed where he stood, stupefied. It was Devyani coming down from the chariot! Why has she come? There was no information before hand. Supposing he had gone out of the ashram, then?

She looked huffed. Was she all right? Meanwhile she came to the sage and touched his feet. He looked at her face with concern. "Are you all right, my dear? You should have informed me of your visit. What is the hurry about? Is there anything wrong?"

By this time they had entered the inner apartment. After some formalities, she came to the point that had kept her agitated and denied the night's sleep. She told him about the illicit relations between the king and Sharmistha, going on for years. Both of them were culprits and they deserved punishment.

"My dear, in my opinion the girl in question is less at fault. She is a poor employee of the palace. She could come under any official's pressure. Any one could take advantage of her position. She is young, she is charming. She is alone too. King Yayati is the real culprit. He is at fault.'

"Yes father, I too think on the same line. He has transgressed the limits enjoined by the marriage on a spouse. He did not mind the solemn oaths taken at the time. Along with him, I want that girl also punished."

"No dear, she had her own limitations. I have already given my opinion about her. Right, what do you want now?"

"Father dear, do whatever you think proper. But let him have a harsh punishment which he remembers for the whole of his life. I don't want him to be dealt with leniently. He should pay for cheating his wife, your dear daughter. He is guilty of breaking his promise."

"All right dear, as you wish. Let him be sent for." He then asked one of her attendants to go back to the palace and pray to the king to visit the ashram at the earliest convenience. The horsemen returned.

Around the noon a messenger came to the king and passed on the message of the sage. Yayati could not believe that Devyani would take the matter out side the four walls of the palace. It was a matter between husband and wife. Why should she drag the old man into the quarrel? As for his relations with Sharmistha, he had already explained his stand, his privileges, the prevalent customs etc, but she won't listen to any. She was too capricious, funny, short-tempered and immature. Now that she had gone to the ashram, the matter might take an unpleasant turn. He had no idea what it could be. He sat down in his chamber and thought over the consequences. He had still some time left for the journey to the ashram.

Late afternoon he set out for the ashram with some of his horsemen. He might send them back if there was a delay. When he reached there, he found the sage waiting for him. It was worrisome and alerted the king. However, he got down from his chariot and wanted to know why the sage had sent for him. He touched the Guru's feet. Then without losing any time the sage took him inside where his wife was seated. Both looked at each other. Anger was still visible in her eyes.

Without losing any time the sage charged him with debauchery and violating the marriage oath. He also said that the king had acted like a thief and set a bad instance for his people. What will the people say if they found that their ruler himself indulged in illicit relationship with an unmarried palace maid, and had kids through her? What sort of example was he setting before his subject?

The king cited the customary privileges of kings having more than one wife and so on. He had done nothing wrong. It was his time-honoured privilege. The sage could have objections if he had neglected his wives. As for Devyani, she had been accorded undue favour in the hierarchy of the queens. This had been a cause of heart-burning among other queens who had been superseded by her. If any one had the right to be displeased, it is those queens and not Devyani for following the privileges. To be frank, she was enjoying more privileges than others although she belonged to another caste.

May be, it was socially higher, but our ancestors have ruled that wedlock out side the fold was not acceptable. Honourable sir, you too are aware of the condition. You yourself performed certain rituals before our marriage to overcome the ruling.

The sage looked at his daughter. There was no change in her mood. He was convinced with the arguments preferred by the king. There was nothing wrong in what he had said. But he was irked by the point that his daughter was married outside her fold, which was a sort of social stigma. This had irritated him. He looked at Devyani again. She looked unmoved and seemed to be asking him not to be softened by his convincing arguments. He deserved a harsh punishment and that should be given.

The sage could not go against the wishes of his daughter. She had been his weakness and would do anything to keep her happy. Therefore, he said, "O king, overcome by passions and carnal desires, you became blind and kept on with illicit relations with an unwed maid. You never thought what impact your deeds would have on your subject. Such was your fascination for the fair sex. I therefore, curse you that from this moment you would be reduced to the state of a decrepit old man, bent with age and disease. That would put an end to your carnal desires. This state would last until some one else offers you his youth on loan."

And lo, the handsome form of the king was transformed into an old man bent with age and disease. Yayati begged of the sage on his bended knees not to be so harsh with his curse, but he was not to be moved. Yayati would have to wait for some one to swipe his youth with his old age.

The sight of the ugly transformation of her 'once beloved husband' (whom she had married by pressurizing her father), stabbed her. 0, what a blunder she had committed in her state of rage! It was the same as she had ruled that Sharmistha should be her slave. Her uncontrollable rage had totally consumed and destroyed her. How would she spend her life with that old, haggard? But the change was irreversible. Was she not responsible for this curse? Tears welled up in her helpless eyes. But it was in vain. The impact of the curse was irreversible. With a loud shriek, she fainted……..